HORRORS AND HAUNTINGS
IN CORNWALL

Companion volume to

Horrors and Hauntings in Devon

HORRORS AND HAUNTINGS
IN CORNWALL

An Anthology of Short Stories

Edited by

William Garnett

TABB HOUSE

First published 1989
Tabb House, 7 Church Street, Padstow, Cornwall

ISBN 0 907018 74 2

Typeset by Exe Valley Dataset Ltd, Exeter, Devon
Printed in Great Britain by
The Guernsey Press Co. Ltd, Guernsey, Channel Islands

Table of Contents

Foreword

In bringing together this collection in two volumes of hitherto unpublished material the Editor has cast his net wide. Some geographic limit had of course to be set and that is conveniently provided by the counties of Devon and Cornwall. Quite wide enough: for even within this rocky and windswept peninsula a remarkable fecundity is evident in the field of the ghostly, the weird, and the grisly.

What connecting thread there may be between the divers elements of these two books is left to the reader to decide; at least he cannot complain of a lack of variety from which to choose, for apart from the range of subject there are the differing angles of approach of our authors, who include one poet.

Ghosts may come in many forms and guises: this much is well authenticated. Those of us who frequent auction sales are perhaps familiar with 'ghost bids', but did you know that a dead man may, under special circumstances, sign a legal will? There are other questions too: In order that a prophecy or a preordained purpose be fulfilled must a ghost appear thrice, or are two appearances sufficient? Can a ghost drop a scrap of paper, or a linen handkerchief into our time? What power have certain works of art over ghosts, or over life itself? Such questions are addressed in these pages, and some receive answers.

Yet mysteries remain. Some of the deeper mysteries, and arguably the grisliest, surround death where no element of the paranormal is present, and this type is included here under the general heading of 'Horrors'. Under 'Hauntings', apart from the phantasms already referred to, must fall those creatures of legend which, though they lead mortals astray – even to their doom – are not themselves manifestations of mortality: of such we have sirens, pixies and a mermaid. Which raises another interesting question: Do mermaids and pixies speak the same language?

It remains only to be said that while some of what is described here is not wholly imaginary, no guarantee of accuracy even in matters of substance is extended to the reader on behalf of either the publisher, the editor or the authors themselves.

The Ghost of Miss Lavinia Little

A. Leigh

ANITA JARMAN paused at a crossroads and then pointed the bonnet of her little red Renault down a lane so narrow that the scrubby oaks leaning across the road from one of its banks came close to those on the further side, making an almost complete roof. She had no idea of how long she had been circling about in the lanes of North Devon and Cornwall, since a moment at Sheepwash where she had appropriately found herself marooned in the midst of a stationary flock of sheep ... But the map and her directions made her believe she was not far from her destination, and she had been told that Trewurgett was at the bottom of a hill. 'If only this was the right hill!' she thought. She was beginning to feel tired and apprehensive. An Alice-in-Wonderland feeling was coming over her that she had strayed into a country where the unexpected always happened and it was impossible to attain one's object – a never-never land. Never, never . . . . She shivered. It had seemed such a good idea, a few days ago, to have a holiday in the country by herself, away from John, and her friends who were all so eager to interfere with unwanted advice and ideas. But now, what would she do with herself in this strange place – if she ever found it – alone, for a week?

Under its banks, the twisting lane was dark; it must be getting late, she thought. At the furthest bend, as far away as she could see, was a figure. 'Good,' she thought; 'I can stop and ask how far it is to Trewurgett.' – It was evidently a woman, a greyish blur standing by the trunk of a beech tree that spread its young, green-leaved branches high across the lane. Anita's glance passed from the distance to the road immediately in front of her and back again, and in that moment the figure had gone. 'That's odd!' she thought. 'She must have moved round the corner.' – But when she reached the corner, no one was ahead of her and there was no cottage doorway nor turning nor gate through which she might have stepped. 'It's very odd!' Anita thought. 'It must have been a trick of the light that confused me.' – But the incident made her situation seem even more Alice-like, and she wished it hadn't happened.

She was relieved to find a moment later that she was coming out of the trees, and that ahead of her was a group of white-washed, grey-slated cottages signed Trewurgett. Then the business of parking the car and knocking on doors and being shown into her 'holiday let' made her forget the grey-faced, grey-skirted vanishing woman. Another woman, a real, substantial, dark-haired person, showed her into Jasmine Cottage.

"I ordered bread and milk for 'ee; tis on the table cos that there pantry's a bit geevy. And if there's anything else you want at all, you've only to tell me," she said, and then: "Ave 'ee had a good journey? – Come from London, I believe? – And staying for a week, by yourself? – Well, I hope you'll have a good time; there isn't many entertainments at Trewurgett, but you can drive to Bude for the cinema and cafés and that sort of thing."

"I'd rather be on my own," Anita found herself saying. "I wanted a holiday away from lots of other people – and there are cafés and cinemas in London, you know."

"Oh, I daresay, though I don't suppose they have so many tourists to keep amused as we do. 'Tis terrible you know, how the people drive around looking for something to do – proper emmets, all over the place."

"What are emmets?" Anita asked, smiling.

"Ants, o' course!"

"Ants! Oh well, like any ant, I expect I shall find plenty to do," she said, for it was a little humiliating to be classed as an ordinary tourist, and she had brought books to read and even some embroidery. If it was warm enough, she would take it out and sit in the garden that she could see outside the window.

"Well my dear, I'll look in again in the morning and see if you're all right."

"Thank you very much – though I'm sure I'll be fine. Goodnight."

Mrs Bluett – for that was her name – took herself off, and Anita was left alone in the little sitting-room. She had already looked about, at the round Victorian table with four chairs in the middle of the room, the horse-hair sofa, white curtains hung from a heavy wooden pole at the window, and black marble clock on the mantlepiece in front of a Victorian looking-glass. She went across the room to open the window and then returned to the fireplace where she stood leaning on her elbows, looking into the glass, where she could see herself – really quite Victorian too, she thought, with her long hair put up to be out of her way while driving – and behind her own face, the window with a green bank outside and daffodils almost incandescent in the dusk, and dark trees. As the room grew darker she stood, listening to the sound of a rushing stream, and the clear voice of a blackbird. Vaguely melancholy was her feeling now, more like Edgar Allen Poe with his perpetual 'Nevermore' than Alice, she thought. Yet as she absorbed the atmosphere of the place a comforting peacefulness crept over her, and a feeling – a feeling that there was someone else in the room with her. She looked up into the glass again, startled; and there reflected was the glimmer of the window and inside, in the dim room, a pale, grey figure. She turned, but as she did so, realised her mistake; she should have held her ground and had a good look at whatever it was that by now would have vanished. And certainly, when she looked not at a reflection but straight through the room to the window, she saw no one and nothing but the white curtains and the furniture that she had noticed before.

'I'm tired,' she thought. 'I must have mistaken one of the white curtains for a pale figure.' – She turned and looked into the glass again, but the curtain on the left-hand side where she thought she had seen someone looked like folds of inanimate stuff and not in the least like a human figure.

She was more disturbed now than she had been after the first disappearance, yet she wasn't frightened, she told herself firmly. All the same, she went into the kitchen to get herself some supper, and although searching for pots and pans and cutlery and discovering how the calor gas stove worked removed her unease, she ate her sausages at the kitchen table rather than in the sitting-room.

While she ate, her thoughts turned to John – and she was rather pleased with herself that they hadn't been with him, obsessively, from the moment she reached the cottage. For she had feared that a holiday by herself in Cornwall would mean that she would be haunted by him the whole time, so that she would come away needing him more than at the beginning; and on her journey, after she got lost at Sheepwash, she had found herself wishing that she had gone somewhere she knew like Sardinia or Torremolinos. But evidently, a ghost was enough to exorcise him – temporarily, at least; for now she wished that he was with her.

The reason for her holiday was that John had told her they must separate: he had to go back to his wife, for the sake of their children. "Nonsense," she had answered. "If you love me you won't give me up; you will make your wife understand that she has got to share you with me."

"I am utterly miserable already; do you really hate me, that you want to make me even more unhappy – to pile misery on misery?"

And she had replied: "I don't know," because it had seemed intolerable that he, who had sworn that he loved her, and had done much to prove it, should now appear to find that life would be easier without her than with her.

"I'll be away for a few weeks so we won't be able to see each other; it will give you time to get used to the idea. Then we can talk about it again."

"I don't want to talk about it, ever."

"If that is your final decision, there's no more to be said. – Goodnight."

He had got up and gone, and in the next few days she had realised that he meant what he said, and that something very terrible had happened, that would not undo itself by being ignored. So she had come to the decision, while he was out of London, that she would go away herself, somewhere she would be quite alone and have time to think. She had been able to arrange the holiday easily and everybody had been very sympathetic, and had said of course she needed a break, but when she came back she would find everything would be all right, for she and John were sure to find a way of getting round their problem. And now, sitting in this quaint old cottage, she found herself wishing, wishing with all her might, as she used to do when she was a child and when the mere force of her desire had seemed sufficient reason for its gratification, that everything would be all right.

Presently the intensity of her thought slackened and she got up from the table to clear away the supper things. But when she ran the hot water tap, only cold came out. "Blast!" she said, and went to look for the water heater. Then, having found and turned on an immersion heater, and finished unloading her car, she went for a stroll through the village. She walked as far as the occasional street lights went, past a pub and a church and a shop, until she came to a humped stone bridge over the stream that she had heard flowing past Jasmine Cottage. Then after watching the quivering light reflected on the surface of the black water below her, she walked back to the inn, and smiling at its name *The Queen and Railway* and wondering where the railway was, she went inside. It wasn't much of a place indoors, with none of the polished brass and coloured lights she had expected, but there was quite a handful of customers leaning over the bar and talking. They stopped and turned to look at her as she came in, which she found disconcerting, but after she had perched on a bar stool and ordered a bourbon that they hadn't got, she found herself comfortably settled with a whisky in her hand.

"It's a lovely evening," she said to the barmaid.

"Ah, but we do need rain."

"I hope not while I'm here."

"You're staying here, then? – At Jasmine Cottage, maybe?"

"Yes."

"What do you make of it there? – On your own, are you?"

"Yes, I am. – It's a dear little place – but tell me, have you ever heard anything about it being haunted?"

"Being haunted, did you say?" – The barmaid looked at one of her customers, who nodded knowingly at her. "George here says they do say there was a ghost – but mind you, all these old places have ghosts; best not take any notice of 'em. – But you're there by yourself, you say?"

"Yes I am, but I've never been frightened by the thought of ghosts."

"All the same," said George, "'tis a bit eerie, on your own, like."

"Go on with you," said the barmaid, in defence of Anita. "A girl's got better things to do than worry about ghosts, hasn't she?"

Anita laughed. "But what sort of ghost is it?"

There was a silence; the barmaid picked up a glass and polished it vigorously, and Anita thought some of the men looked a little embarrassed.

"Well, seeing as none of us do believe in ghosties, we needn't bother our heads with it," said another customer.

"Quite right," George answered. He put down his tankard with finality. "I'm on my way now, me dears. I've got to get up early to sow another row of me taters tomorrow; so goodnight, all."

There was a chorus of goodnights and a general move to the door, and then Anita was left alone with the barmaid, and a boy and a girl in a dark corner.

"Do you believe in ghosts?" Anita asked.

The barmaid looked at her. "I can't say I do, never having seen one. But if I did, then maybe I'd change my mind."

"That's just what I would have said . . . But do tell me more about the ghost at Jasmine Cottage."

Again there was a pause, before the barmaid said: "I believe it's a grey woman who flits about the place . . ."

"A grey woman!" Anita was astonished by this corroboration of the experience that she had thought was probably only the product of her tired imagination. "But she's not a frightening apparition, I hope?"

"I never heard of anyone being frightened by her. George says she's a Miss Lavinia Little who lived there – ever such a long time ago, before his grandmother's time. – But you haven't seen her yourself, have you?"

"I think I must have done. I saw a grey figure when I was driving down the lane this evening, and again in the sitting-room later on. It seemed to fit your description of a grey woman flitting about the place."

"Fancy that!" the woman said with what seemed to Anita exaggerated surprise before adding in a more level tone. "I mean, just fancy seeing a ghost twice in a day and I've never even seen one – Well, I hope you don't see her again."

"Why not? – She seemed quite harmless."

"Maybe so – but to tell you the truth, I don't like these ghosts and spooks – they don't seem natural."

Again there was a curious change of tone in the barmaid's voice. Anita's curiosity was now thoroughly aroused, but the woman would say no more on the subject. Anita finished her drink and made a move towards the door, thinking as she walked home that she looked forward almost eagerly to the possibility of seeing Miss Lavinia Little again.

The next morning was fine, however, and Anita did not think about ghosts. Instead she looked at the map, and drove off quite early, to see Boscastle and Tintagel.

While she was away, entertaining herself with the sights of Cornwall, the inhabitants of Trewurgett derived some entertainment from discussing her.

Mrs Bluett had met Susie Barnes the barmaid in the shop that morning. "What do you make of your new visitor?" Susie asked.

"She seems a nice girl; quiet, mind you. You don't get much out of her."

"Well, she came into the bar last night and sat herself down as bold as brass – and asked if there's a ghost at Jasmine Cottage! It just happened that George had been talking about it; he said it was a funny thing, a maid coming on her own to stay like that – and he said she'd better keep her eyes shut or she might get cursed by Miss Lavinia Little. Of course, we all told him not to talk such old nonsense, but just at that moment, in she came. And I can tell you, she gave me quite a turn when the first thing she did was to ask about ghosts! – And it does seem odd, her being on her own like that; it isn't natural, at her age. She must have had a row with her boyfriend, or something."

"I daresay you're right; she didn't seem interested at all in having company when I talked to her last evening; but all I know about her is that she comes from London."

"Does she, then? – You wouldn't think someone from London would be taken in by ghosts! – She said she'd seen it twice; once coming down the lane, and once in the lounge."

"No! – Did she? – She'd best not see it again, anyway!"

"I expect she just imagined the whole thing."

Mrs Bluett agreed, but even so the story was soon round most of the village that the solitary young visitor at Jasmine Cottage had seen the ghost.

"Poor maid!" said George to his wife that night when he had relayed the story home from the pub.

"Just goes to show; being rich isn't everything," she replied placidly, going on with her knitting.

"Well, all ways, she's only seen her twice," George added in the young woman's defence.

In the afternoon a further event connected with Anita sent a ripple of interest through the village. Mr Pick, the innkeeper, got a telephone call from a gentleman in London asking if Miss Jarman at Jasmine Cottage could be contacted, as there was an important message for her.

"You'd best give me the message, and I'll see it's delivered," Mr Pick said.

The speaker rather reluctantly agreed, and in due course Mr Pick went up the road with a piece of paper in his hand. Jasmine Cottage was firmly shut, and he went round to Mrs Bluett. "Give it to me," she said. "If you put it through the letter-box under that old curtain she may not see it, but I'll give it to her as soon as she gets back."

The paper was handed over and Mrs Bluett scanned it eagerly. "Could be a brother, I suppose, but more likely her young man."

Anita drove that morning first to Tintagel, the home of King Arthur, and King Mark the husband of Tristan's Isolde; a fine place for star-crossed lovers. But magnificent as Tintagel Castle was with its towering cliffs, decayed battlements and amethyst and blue and green sea wrinkled round its knees, she liked Boscastle better. For here there were also great cliffs rising out of the spray, but at the end of the dramatic inlet from the sea was a comfortable, homely village, and however romantic a cliff-top perch might be, a warm nest of a home was more desirable. She had lunch outside a pub between Tintagel and Boscastle, and after seeing Boscastle broke her drive to walk through a wood where she found a sunny sheltered clearing with primroses and a few wood-anemones growing among tangles of dead grass and brambles. While sitting on a tree-stump in the sun she heard a cuckoo calling, and in that moment the world appeared transformed, as if her senses had acquired a new, expanded faculty of experience, so that the warmth of the sun, the sights and scents of the scene before her and the sound of birdsong came together as one harmonious expression of joy.

She returned to Jasmine Cottage that evening with a great feeling of well-being, and as she let herself into the house, thought that she would celebrate with a half-bottle of champagne she had brought with her, to keep company with a piece of steak she had got in Camelford.

She had only been indoors a moment when Mrs Bluett appeared.

"I've got a message for you," she said. "It came to Mr Pick down at the local," and she held out a scrap of paper.

Anita took it and read it quickly: 'Meet me tomorrow for lunch the Clarence Exeter urgent ring me tonight John'.

Anita looked at Mrs Bluett with a radiant face to thank her; and it was with regret that Mrs Bluett watched her go into the public telepone box down the road, where there was no chance of the conversation being overheard.

In the box, Anita got onto John's number quickly, and he answered at once, evidently having been waiting at his office for the call.

"Thank heavens you've rung!" he said. "I've been in a fearful state. Now listen carefully; I've found that life is utterly impossible without you, but there's only one way to stay together, and that is by getting right away, somewhere safe from Jo, where she'll never find us. So if you say yes, I'll chuck my job, and then we'll have to be patient until I've found something else. Then we'll go off together – for ever. Will you do it?"

This was what Anita wanted more than anything in the world, to have John completely to herself. The whys and wherefores did not at this moment of triumph seem important. "Of course I'll do it. I'll go anywhere in the world with you."

"Thank God for that! – And thank you, darling! – But you will come tomorrow? – There's a lot to be arranged, and I don't think we'd better meet in London for the time being."

"Yes, of course I'll meet you in Exeter."

"Goodbye until tomorrow."

Anita went back to the cottage, and found Mrs Bluett still there. "I've brought you a pasty, my dear," she said. "I don't know if you've got anything for your supper, but I thought you might be hungry."

"How very kind of you. But as a matter of fact, I did get something for tonight. But I can take your pasty when I go tomorrow, can't I? – It will keep?"

"Oh yes, it will keep a few days – but you aren't leaving us already are you?"

"I'm afraid I shall have to. I've been called back to London – but I've loved this place, so maybe I'll come back one day."

"You've liked it inspite of the ghost, have you?"

Anita laughed. "How did you know I'd seen a ghost?"

"Oh – things get around. But I hope you won't be bothered with it again."

"Why not? – It didn't bother me, you know; in fact, I'd rather like to see it again."

"I shouldn't do that, my dear."

"Why ever not?"

"It's only an old story I know, and probably not a word of truth in it, but they do say that Miss Lavinia Little shows herself three times to girls who are never going to wed, Miss Little having been crossed in love three times herself, they say. There now; that's the long and the short of it, and nothing but an old wives' tale, it be, too."

Anita laughed once more. "Well, thank you for telling me. If I see her again, I shan't let it worry me; but I don't suppose I will, you know."

"I'm sure you're right. Goodnight, m'love."

Once again Anita was left alone in the cottage, but inspite of Mrs Bluett's warning, she felt no forebodings tonight. She laid a place for herself in the sitting-room and lit the electric fire in front of the cast-iron grate. She rummaged in the kitchen cupboards and was rewarded by finding some wine glasses. If only John were here with her tonight, she thought. But tomorrow she would see him again, so much sooner than she had expected, and for a so much better reason. So after all, everything was going to be all right!

She ate her supper and then sat with her embroidery and the last of the champagne, thinking about the events of the day. First there had been her outing to the wonderful scenery on the coast, and then she had come back to this adorably romantic cottage to find John's message, and actually speak to him on the phone, so that now she could sit, comfortably replete from her steak and wine, with the warming thought that soon they would be together – for ever. It had been one of the most memorable days of her life, and if she were never happy again, she would still have that to remember. At this thought, she was surprised; for why should she think it, when her happiness had only just begun?

The next day was dull and grey, disappointingly and un-expectedly so, after the brilliance of the previous one. And Anita now found herself assailed by the doubts that had not occurred to her in the happiness of the night before. Did John really think he could escape from his wife? Did he really want to? And did he really intend to abandon his children? These questions that had seemed unnecessary last night, presented themselves with an ominous negative reply tolling after each. But at least, Anita thought as she got into the car and drove away, she hadn't seen the ghost again!

Mrs Bluett, standing at her kitchen window, watched the visitor leave. She was sorry to see her go as she had liked the young woman, and wished she had been able to find out just why she had come to Cornwall by herself and now had to meet someone in Exeter. It was galling that through her authority as caretaker of Jasmine Cottage, she had not found out more about her.

She watched the car go up the lane and then, to her surprise, return a few minutes later. The key had been left under a stone; Miss Jarman retrieved it, unlocked the door and went inside. 'I wonder what for?' Mrs Bluett wondered.

Anita had returned because she had indeed forgotten some-thing; her embroidery, which was still in the sitting-room where she had left it the previous evening. She went into the sitting-room. There, standing to the left of the window, was a woman, wearing a long grey dress and some sort of cap on her head. Her expression was severe, but somehow not unfriendly. Anita looked at her in astonishment, unable to think of anything to say. The woman bowed her head slightly and then, instead of moving, as Anita expected, she disappeared.

Anita sat down in a chair suddenly, feeling dizzy. Some minutes later Mrs Bluett came in, and found her sitting there, looking rather white and dazed, not at all like the gay young woman she had been the night before.

"Are you feeling ill?" she asked, sympathetically.

"I felt a bit faint – but I think I'm better now."

Mrs Bluett was full of concern. "I saw you coming back, and wondered if anything had happened. Can I get you anything? A drink?"

"No, thank you, I'm truly all right now. I must be going." Anita gave Mrs Bluett a weak smile. "I musn't forget that; it's what I really came back for," she said, picking up her embroidery. "Goodbye once again!"

For the last time, Anita drove away, 'She didn't come back because she was feeling ill, then. That must have come on in here. It's that dratted Miss Lavinia Little, I suppose!' Mrs Bluett thought.

ANITA, when she reached Exeter rather late, was not altogether surprised to find that John was not waiting for her, and while she waited through the afternoon with an increasingly heavy heart, she knew that, wait as long as she might, he would not come.

The Mistress of Vellandower

Walter Walkham

"THE sort of place you're looking for," said the young house-agent, "only comes on the market once in a blue moon."

"What?" said Roger. "Even in Cornwall?"

"Yes: even in Cornwall – especially in Cornwall. It would probably be much quicker for you to acquire a site and build."

"All the best sites have been built on already," grumbled Roger.

"Ah!" said the house-agent. "I can think of one that's available. Has anyone offered you Vellandower yet?"

"No. I don't remember the name."

The agent searched in the cupboard behind his desk and, producing a sheaf of papers, handed Roger and Betty each a typewritten description of Vellandower.

He explained "The house was gutted by fire fifty years ago, and never re-built. The owner died last year, and his executors are selling. Perhaps you'd like to read the details."

After a minute's study, Betty murmured "A Georgian house."

"A complete ruin, I'm afraid," said the agent, "but the buyer will get a magnificent site."

"Who," asked Betty, "were this Basset family who built it?"

"Very important people in the seventeenth and eighteenth centuries: land-owners, mineral owners, politicians. The Vellandower branch ran to daughters, so the name died out – at least at Vellandower – during the eighteen nineties. The Bassets had been there well over a hundred years."

"Do you happen to know," asked Betty, "if the place is haunted?"

Roger stirred petulantly in his seat, finding it difficult to read about the property while Betty chattered.

The agent, sensing Roger's irritation, lowered his voice, addressing only Betty.

"There is a legend about a Vellandower ghost, going back to eighteen ninety-five, when the predecessors to my firm offered the place at auction. The sale was held at the Angel Hotel across the street. Would you care to hear about it?"

"Yes, please," said Betty eagerly.

"Well, the story goes that the bidding was just about done, and the property on the point of being knocked down, when a female voice very gently but very imperiously said 'One hundred pounds more!'

"There was a commotion, and everyone looked around to see the new bidder, but there wasn't a woman in the room.

"The auctioneer asked 'Whose bid was that, please?'

"The same voice said 'The mistress of Vellandower.'

"The gathering broke up in disorder, and Vellandower remained for sale for forty years."

"Humph!" said Roger, who had stopped reading. "A ghost bidding at an auction! I wonder how she would have paid!"

"I can't vouch for the story," said the agent, with a hint of apology. "It was a bit before my time."

"Who was this mistress of Vellandower?" asked Betty.

"According to the legend, it was the last heiress, a Miss Basset. On her death-bed, she is supposed to have bemoaned the lack of a Basset heir to Vellandower. She was determined it should stay in the family."

Roger referred again to the particulars, and read aloud "... the avenue extending to the river bank and lined by double rows of mature beeches, etcetera ... etcetera ... extending in all to some fifteen acres."

"Or thereabouts," added the agent.

"I'd like to see it," said Roger with sudden decision. "Can we make an appointment to view?"

"There's no need for an appointment. And no key. I'll show you where it is on the map ..."

ROGER switched off his car engine and waited patiently for the last cow to saunter off the lane, and pass through the gateway to the milking yard.

"Thank you!" the farmer called out, waving his stick.

Roger thrust his head through the car window.

"I suppose we are right for Vellandower?" he asked.

Closing the gate on his cows, the farmer approached the car inquisitively.

"That's right," he said. "Straight ahead. The road don't go nowhere else. Interested in the property, then, are you?"

"I might be."

"Left it a bit late, haven't you?"

"You mean it's sold?"

"No, no, no! I mean, 'tis a bit late in the day: not long before dark."

"Is that important?"

"Well, I dunno," replied the farmer, scratching his chin reflectively. "I haven't met no-one who've been to Vellandower 'cept in broad daylight, not for years . . . Well, good luck to you."

He shook his head mysteriously and turned back to the yard gate. Roger re-started the car engine.

Soon the lane passed between massive masonry gate-posts, one of them bearing a For Sale notice. Beyond the posts, on either side of the lane the land had reverted to natural forest.

"These are the paddocks we're passing through now," announced Roger.

"What paddocks?" demanded Betty.

"You didn't read the particulars: 'From the entrance gateway' – note that 'gateway'; there are no gates – 'the carriage drive passes between the paddocks to a car park at the rear of the house site.' "

"So," said Betty, "we are now going along the carriage drive!"

"Right. And here is the car park." Roger pulled up and added "If the executors, or somebody hadn't commissioned a jungle clearance scheme, there wouldn't have been any carriage drive, or car park either."

Roger got out of the car and walked towards a ruinous wall. Reluctantly, Betty followed. Together they picked their way across the house site, now a pile of rubble, with only quoins and chimney-breasts standing a few feet above ground.

"If it caught fire," asked Betty, "why isn't it all blackened?"

"The weather's had time to wipe out all signs of charring," explained Roger. "You see that sycamore – there, look, growing out of what used to be a fireplace – that can't be less than thirty years old, judging by the size of it."

Betty shivered.

"Haven't you seen enough?" she asked.

"No. Having come this far, we might as well have a look round."

"I can't think why you're interested."

"Fifteen acres of land: that's why I'm interested. Do you know how much a plot of land costs in Greater London or Birmingham, just big enough to build a three-bedroomed detached house and garage on?"

"I've no idea. And I don't care. I don't like this place one little bit."

"Well, now I'm here," declared Roger, "I'm going to have a look at the beech-lined avenue leading to the river bank. Are you coming, or will you go back to the car?"

"I'll come with you," said Betty, taking his arm.

The jungle clearance scheme had been extended to the terrace fronting the house, and the avenue beyond. Roger stood on the terrace and gasped at the vista.

"Marvellous!" he said. "What a site!"

Betty waited for him to feast his eyes. Then she said, "Well, you've seen it. Can we go now?"

"I'm going down to the river. Are you coming?"

Betty moved closer to Roger, and they descended a flight of overgrown steps to the grass terrace. In the long grass they stumbled on the stumps of recently-felled trees, some of them more than twelve inches across.

In the gathering dusk, the avenue seemed very wide and long. Roger led the way to the splendid beeches on the west side. Between the two rows lay depressions which had once been ornamental ponds; a few of these still held water, which reflected the autumnal foliage of the beeches. Roger started to calculate in his mind the costs of restoring the avenue and the ponds, and building a neo-Georgian house . . .

At the river bank, he watched and listened as the trout rose for flies until the light failed them; and then he looked back at the magnificent avenue, imagining his new house standing at the far end. Betty stood like a statue under the nearest beech.

As Roger returned to her, a night breeze sighed through the

trees. Betty started on seeing him, and reached out to clasp his arm. Her face was blanched.

"Oh!" she breathed. "Take me back to the car!" Her breath came quick and shallow.

"What is it?" asked Roger. "You look as if you've seen a ghost!"

"Come on," she sobbed. "The car."

ROGER waited for Betty to explain, in her own good time, the fright she had experienced. Only after they had put two miles of lanes between them and Vellandower did she relax sufficiently to talk, and then in an unnaturally querulous voice.

"I saw her," she said.

"Saw whom?"

"The mistress of Vellandower. She was wearing a long grey trailing dress, very small at the waist, and a dark shawl around her shoulders, with a grey bonnet. She walked slowly, leaning on a stick. The funny thing was, the trees seemed to bow to her as she passed, and when she stopped opposite one, it bowed so low its branches almost touched the ground."

"Good heavens!" said Roger. "Didn't its trunk groan a bit?"

"There was absolute silence – until the grey lady started rummaging in the dead leaves with her stick. Then the leaves clinked like metal, and shone, too, like gold. Then when she stopped at the pond nearest the river, the water ruffled as if it was boiling, just by her staring at it. Then she came nearer and stared at me . . ."

Betty paused and Roger asked her "What did she look like?"

"Under that bonnet, there was just a skull . . . I was petrified."

Roger slowed the car and murmured, "Yes . . . I bet you were . . . Was that when you spoke to me?"

"No. A breeze came up first and rustled the trees, and the . . . the person seemed to just vanish. I thought she'd turned me to stone. Then I reached out and grabbed you, and I managed to find my voice."

Roger accelerated and said "Now we know why the locals only go there in broad daylight . . . That agent fellow: he knows a lot more about this place than he told us. I'm going to talk to him tomorrow . . ."

HAVING Roger's assurance that he had not the slightest intention of purchasing Vellandower, Betty went shopping while he called on the house-agent.

The agent greeted Roger breezily.

"Good morning! What did you think of Vellandower?"

"I was impressed."

"Isn't it a wonderful site?" said the agent. "I can't think of a more idyllic setting for a country house, can you?"

"One thing bothers me, though," said Roger. "You haven't told us the whole story of the place yet, have you?"

"How do you mean?"

"Yesterday you took us up to eighteen ninety-five. What happened after that?"

"The house remained empty until Mr Maclean bought it in the mid-thirties."

"The Mr Maclean whose executors are selling it now?"

"That's right. He died last year in his native Scotland. I understand he was ninety-six."

"How long did he occupy Vellandower?"

"Oh, not very long."

"Long enough to put right forty years of dilapidations?"

"Yes. He had that done before he moved in."

"How long after he moved in did the fire occur?"

The agent blinked and swallowed before replying.

"The story goes that the fire broke out the very night after he had taken up residence."

"The mistress of Vellandower didn't like him, then, did she?" said Roger. "Or was it Mrs Maclean she objected to?"

"Mrs Maclean never saw Vellandower. Mr Maclean came here as a young – or young middle-aged widower."

"Had he any family?"

"One teen-aged daughter. Mr Maclean was said to have been extremely proud of her."

"And he intended to make her the mistress of Vellandower?"

"I suppose so."

"And what happened to her?"

Sheepishly the agent replied: "She perished in the fire."

The Lady in Brown

Walter Walkham

BOSTENNACK has only been an elderly persons' home for the last twenty years or so. I can remember the last of the Lerryns living there, until the mid-thirties.

The Lerryns had occupied Bostennack for over a hundred years. In fact, they built the place in the early 1800s, having made money out of tin – not by mining it, but by collecting royalties. A cumbersome granite place they built, with more substance than grace about its architecture, but they lived in style, with house servants and gardeners.

Then suddenly the old bachelor, Mr Francis Lerryn, decided to go and live somewhere in the Greek islands, and the servants found themselves out of work. Bostennack was empty for a year or two, and we schoolboys used to hunt rabbits in the neglected grounds, with airgun, ferret, and net.

We had to stop rabbiting, of course, when Bostennack was let to some people called Blazenby. There was nothing Cornish about the Blazenbys, but, as we said at the time, they were very nice people all the same. They came from somewhere in the Midlands, bringing a couple of servants with them.

One evening in the autumn, Mother was preening herself excitedly – Father said she was "aeriated" – because Mrs Blazenby had invited her to tea the following day, putting her one up on the rest of the Townswomen's Guild.

"I never thought," she told Father, "I'd live to see the day I'd take tea up at Bostennack! Mark's invited, too, as company for Mrs Blazenby's son. Mind," said Mother sternly to me, "I'm putting you on your best behaviour, Mark. Remember, you're not to attack the cakes as if you haven't seen food for a fortnight . . ."

INSTEAD of walking up Bostennack's winding drive, I cut a corner and led Mother through the overgrown shrubbery, while she fussed about arriving too early or too late.

Presently I noticed a woman in the shrubbery, only a few yards away. She wore an antiquated, long, brown dress, very wide in the skirt, and a wide, brown bonnet with ribbons. She muttered abusively at something on the other side of a privet hedge, and I stopped walking, fascinated. When she half turned and looked at me, I saw iron-grey curls inside the bonnet and a vicious face that chilled my stomach. She glared at me like the witch in the Grimms' Fairy Tales in our bookcase at home, but only for a moment; then, still grumbling, she bustled away in the direction of the kitchen garden. Relieved, I hurried away after Mother, my legs feeling strangely weak.

A maid admitted us to the house and led us to Mrs Blazenby. It was my first encounter with a lady of Mrs Blazenby's standing, and I was impressed by the way she made us feel at ease in her spacious, elegant drawing-room.

"We won't wait for Arnold," she said, explaining that Arnold was her son. She tugged at the bell-pull beside the mantelshelf.

The tea tray was brought by an elderly manservant with a stoop; his unblinking gaze took in Mother, me and the four corners of the room in one sweep. I thought what a strange household it was, to accommodate both the fierce old lady in the shrubbery and this forbidding old man, now putting down the tray and withdrawing, bent and silent.

Skilfully, our hostess included me in the conversation, so I felt encouraged to ask "Who is the lady I saw in the shrubbery, Mrs Blazenby?"

"Really, Mark!" Mother protested against my boldness.

Mrs Blazenby looked intently at me and asked "Can you describe her?"

As best I could, I described the old lady's Victorian costume, but omitted reference to her evil expression. Our hostess sat stock still.

Mother said "I didn't see anyone in the shrubbery."

"Mark did, though," said Mrs Blazenby quietly. "I know who she is. We thought . . . we hoped, when we came to Cornwall, we'd left her behind. We call her the Lady in Brown . . . Will you have a sandwich, Mark? Or a piece of cake?"

Despite the evident shock of my revelations, which had left Mrs Blazenby deathly pale, she strove to fulfil her duty as a hostess. As for me, I decided that when the time came, Mother and I would go home along the drive, avoiding the shrubbery where I had come face to face with the loathsome old woman.

My heart missed a beat when the door opened, but it was only the gloomy, staring manservant with some hot water for the tea tray. He told Mrs Blazenby in sepulchral tones "Mr Arnold is coming directly, madam."

"Thank you, Todd," said Mrs Blazenby, and I wondered if Todd was a descendant of the demon barber.

After he had left, I had another surprise which made me leap inside my skin: a motionless figure stood silhouetted in the open French window. It was the outline of a young man, and I wondered how long he had stood there, observing us all.

"Arnold!" shrilled Mrs Blazenby, startled, but she quickly recovered her composure and introduced her son to Mother and me.

When Arnold walked into the room so that we could see light and shade on his face, I could hardly believe he was our hostess' son. His hair was silvery white and his face care-worn, the eyes giving him an alert, hunted expression. Despite his smooth skin, he looked all of forty years of age, whereas I had been expecting to meet someone only a year or two more than my sixteen.

I had difficulty in talking to Arnold, because he was apparently not interested in any kind of sport, and unwilling to introduce a topic of his own. Fortunately, Mrs Blazenby kept the conversation flowing, without any help from her son.

Presently at Mrs Blazenby's suggestion Arnold and I went for a stroll in the grounds. All the time Todd watched us from a discreet distance. Still Arnold hardly spoke, and I decided that Bostennack must be the oddest, creepiest household in Cornwall; I was thankful when, after we returned to the drawing-room, Mother said "We really must be going . . ."

MOTHER and I were half way home before we stopped glancing over our shoulders. Even then we hardly spoke, and I suspected that the floodgates of Mother's chatter would not open until she reported to Father on our first social visit to Bostennack.

I was right. Father had to hear all about the pleasant Mrs Blazenby, the dismal Todd and the aged boy, Arnold. I guessed that Mrs Blazenby had told Mother much more about the mysterious Lady in Brown, while Arnold and I had been strolling in the grounds. Mother did not once mention the Lady in Brown, but several times checked her prattle with furtive glances at me; I would not raise the subject, as I knew Father would be sceptical.

After our meal Father helped Mother with the washing-up as usual, and I absented myself, probably to tinker with my bike. When I returned, Mother was talking nineteen to the dozen, and I eavesdropped.

". . . He's only nineteen, but his hair's as white as that plate. It went white overnight a few weeks ago, after he had a terrible fright. Now this man Todd watches over him all the time. Mrs Blazenby said the family is under a curse; they thought it all started with some maidservant who'd been wronged by a Blazenby back in Victorian times. This Lady in Brown that Mark saw is connected with it. Whenever she's seen, the eldest son dies soon afterwards. It's what happened to her husband – Arnold's father."

"Curse indeed!" muttered Father. "There's someone at the bottom of this: flesh and blood, I mean. This is a case for the police."

"Then what do you suppose Mark saw, if it wasn't a ghost?"

"A ghost who walked to Cornwall all the way from the Midlands," scoffed Father. "First time I heard of a ghost as mobile as that. No. You mark my words: this is an inside job. It's one for Inspector Trewin of the County police."

Father's words reassured me. All the same, I was relieved to see in the mirror when I went to bed that my hair had retained its own sort of brown colour. And so it still had the next morning.

As a sixth-form boy reading mathematics, physics and chemistry, I could not reconcile ghosts with the properties of matter, by any natural phenomena known to me. But however hard I tried to deny the existence of the supernatural, the image of the horrible old woman in Bostennack shrubbery would not be dispelled. When I took Grimms' Fairy Tales out of the bookcase and examined the illustration of the witch, I saw a caricature of the Lady in Brown staring at me from the page, and my hair stood on end; the picture frightened me far more than it had done when I was a small boy learning to read.

On the way home from school one evening, I saw Arnold in the light of a shop window. Under a Trilby hat, he looked younger than when I had first met him, yet much older than his nineteen years. I spoke to him; though he answered perfunctorily, I could not be sure he recognised me. He stood there, as though nursing some private sorrow. Then the stooping Todd appeared at Arnold's side and, staring right through me, led him away.

Perhaps Father was right, I thought. Perhaps Todd was, after all, a descendant of Sweeney of that ilk, but more subtle and painstaking in his atrocities; perhaps Todd was the Lady in Brown. Or perhaps the maid was, or someone else . . .

I VISITED Bostennack only once more during the brief Blazenby occupation. Then I was with a group of carol singers collecting for a children's Christmas charity. We called ourselves the Inasmuch, from the Biblical text, 'Inasmuch as ye have done it unto one of these little children . . .' When Father read our name on the collecting-box, he said it meant, "Put insamuch as you can."

Walking up Bostennack drive by torchlight, surrounded by robust young friends, I felt very brave. I wondered how the others would react if the Lady in Brown suddenly confronted us. We reached the house and arranged ourselves on the terrace before the front door.

"Hark the Herald Angels," announced our leader, Tom Soady, and the accompanist gave us a chord from his squeeze-box. There was plenty of space at Bostennack, and to fill it with sound we sang right lustily. Towards the end of the last verse, the door opened, revealing Todd on the threshold of the well-lit hall. Inside stood Mrs Blazenby, and further in on a step-ladder, hammer in hand, the silver-haired Arnold paused in his task of fastening Christmas decorations.

". . . Glory-y to the new-born King," we concluded somewhat distractedly.

"Please come in," Mrs Blazenby invited us.

We trooped in, murmuring our thanks in turn as we each took a glass of sherry from a tray held by Todd, who looked at no-one but saw us all. Tom Soady engaged Mrs Blazenby in conversation while we sipped our sherry. I failed to catch Arnold's eye, as he stood absently on the ladder, apparently awaiting our departure.

Presently Tom called for 'While Shepherds Watched', so we drank the rest of our sherry, returned the glasses to Todd's tray and prepared to sing.

It happened during the second verse, when we reached '. . . for mighty dread had seized their trou-bled mind." We heard a shout, and then Arnold Blazenby and the step-ladder crashed to the floor. Todd put down the tray and flew to Arnold's side. The singers and the accordion petered out in a buzz of apprehension.

Pressing forward, I saw Todd on his knees, sobbing with anxiety. Mrs Blazenby stood nearby, gazing down with horror at a bloodied hammer on the floor at her feet.

"He must have fallen off the ladder," said someone, but I knew better.

Shaking with fright, I peeped through the throng and saw in Todd's lap Arnold's head with blood flowing from a gash across the temple. For the first time in my young life, I looked on the waxen face of Death.

I COULD not mention the Lady in Brown to anyone in the Inasmuch; I would have been branded a superstitious fool. I did not even mention her again to my Mother; Father would only have held me up to ridicule.

Before the Christmas holiday, the police visited and questioned all the Inasmuch individually. They took statements from a few of the senior people. A young detective-constable called and heard me out.

"Mr Jago," he said, and I think it was the first time anyone had 'mistered' me, "did you actually see this Lady in Brown at the time Mr Blazenby was . . . er . . . met his death?"

"No," I admitted. "I didn't."

The officer folded his papers and returned them to his breast pocket, having written down only my full name and the time and date.

"I don't want a statement from you for the time being," he said, "not until I've had a word with the inspector in charge of the case."

"What about Mother?" I asked. "Don't you want to talk to her?"

"Only if the inspector wants a statement from her."

"You don't believe a word I said about the Lady in Brown, do you?"

"Mr Jago, my job is to collect evidence. And superstition isn't evidence." The officer rose, adding, "Thank you for your time, all the same."

I last heard about the Blazenby affair through the newspaper: the coroner had declared that Arnold's death was due to cardiac arrest, as discovered by the County Pathologist.

Soon after the inquest, Mrs Blazenby and her servants left Bostennack. As far as I know, the Lady in Brown left with them.

The Enchantress of Castle Treen

Michael Goodman

HE pulled on the wheel and the Castle Treen rock
Fell to the right, and he thought, "I'll lock
The spokes till we leave the surf behind."
And he put those rocks out of his mind.
He considered where their mackerel lay
And how they would spend much of that day
Threading nets over the side
Of the boat, throwing the barrels wide
That would mark the edge of their fishing place.
So he stared through the gale. It pushed at his face
As it always did with the harbour behind
And the bow wave sprayed him, fanned by the wind.

Then the wheel house window he bolted tight.
They rode high in the water, travelling light
And the fishing boat, jolting, heaved on the swell.
"Good," he thought, "she's riding well.
The gear's tied down. The engine's in tune.
We'll be out to the catch and busy soon."

But he glanced to the right and Castle Treen
Had shifted ahead where it should not have been.
"Strange," he muttered. "The wheel's tied fast
And the current runs true." He looked up at the mast
Where the pennant pointed shoreward still.
It suddenly shuddered. The gale sang shrill
As he hung on the wheel to change the tack
Of the boat. He braced the breadth of his back
On the wall of the wheel house, peering out
Through the salt-grimed glass. "We're going about,"
He said, and to the right the rock moved again
Though bigger it seemed as he watched through the pane
Of the wheel house window. The engine took hold
At a different tone as slantwise they rolled.

His hand worked the boat, demanding more speed
As a jockey might do, seeking the lead
On a gasping racehorse, the finish in sight.
But again Castle Treen lay not to his right
And bigger the rocks were. They could rip
A boat in two. He bit his lip.
At the sight of the foamy sea splashing,
Submerging the black mass, the dashing
Fullness of a grey-green wave
On the dark rocks, marking the grave
Of boats without number, scattered and lost.
He pressed for more speed, but that was the most
They could gain. Perplexed, he tightened his grip
On the edge of the wheel as he felt his craft slip
Into a trough and fall . . . fall away
To a spot where – amazing – a smoother stretch lay
And there they were . . . becalmed.

"Ah," he muttered, "we are off course
From first to last today," yet a force
That he faintly felt, hinted, "Not so."
But what message was this? The boat became slow
As the sound of the engine faded, then ceased,
And the craft, from its pattern, drifted, released.
They wallowed in their calmness, the waves dying,
The soft wind gently sighing.
"What's this?" he asked, leaving the wheel
For the side of the boat. "Strange. I feel . . ."
And he stared, confused, squinting at the shore.
"The sea never calmed this quickly before."
He looked at the rocks. He heard the sound
Of women in chorus, singing a round.
The voices were sweet, yet the words were not plain
So he cupped his right ear to hear them again.
His mates came to join him. They stood at his side
And at last they made out, where the rocks touched the tide,
Three . . . four . . . women there,
Perched on the rocks, slim and fair,
Small of body, moving their arms

With welcoming gestures, beguiling charms.

Men quizzed each other: "Who are those?"
They rubbed their eyes. "I suppose
That this is a dream, and I'm in my bed
And a curious fantasy turns my head,"
One said, while on they drifted, blind
To families they'd left behind,
The other women that they knew,
Girls of Porthcurno, Lamorna too,
Mothers, fathers, children, wives,
And all the things that filled their lives . . .
Nearer . . . nearer . . glistening skin
And limbs . . . They admired, their breath sucked in.

One woman transfixed him, coolly, full
In the face, lips slightly parted. A pool
Of sunlight enveloped her, A scent
Caught his nostrils as he bent
To see her beauty . . . So close they sailed.
He gazed entranced, and deep he inhaled.
Yet something there was which caused him to fear
A danger, hiding somehow here
Behind his pleasure. But hair outspread,
Pale strands in the breeze, she lifted her head
And gave him a look so comforting, warm,
That without knowing why, he dismissed his alarm.
Then with bent finger, she beckoned to him
And her head drew back. Her shoulders slim,
Her arms and breasts and waist he saw,
And filled with desire, seeking more,
He stretched his right arm out to the land,
Gripping the rail with his other hand
And she leaned to him; her eyes were bright
As she held out her arms, graceful and white.

She looked in his eyes. Sweetly she gazed
And he smiled in return, nervous, amazed.
She seemed to say, "My song is for you.

I sing of comfort, friendship too.
Come close. Listen. Give me your hand."
He stretched his fingers towards her and
Nothing inside him warned to keep clear.
He felt the warmth of her hovering near
And powerless he leaned, memories gone
Of the tales that fishermen told. The sun
Shone steadily down on the approaching pair,
Making sparks of the droplets adorning her hair,
As they touched . . . .

"Off Castle Treen was a wreck last night,"
The paper said, "With the dismal sight
Of broken planks and tangled nets
Adrift near rocky tidepools. Let's
Give thanks to the men who catch our fish,
Who risk their lives for our supper dish.
The wreck of the boat had gone aground
But strangely, her men could not be found."

The End of the Holidays

Joan Tyack

LIONEL said afterwards that all the trouble began with Betsy getting stuck down a hole. He said he had felt it in his bones. "But you couldn't have known about the baby," objected Norah. Lionel agreed, but all the same, there had been enough trouble brewing for them that evening one way and another.

Expressly forbidden by the aunts to take Betsy down into the woods, where the lure of fresh rabbit runs was too strong for any terrier to resist, the children had gone off after tea with Jimmy Lobb and his ferret into the steep wood over-hanging the river. Here under the heronry where fishy droppings splattered the leaves of the holly undergrowth, there was an intricate network of runs under the tree roots, and Jimmy had no trouble at all in finding a freshly opened burrow where the rabbit pellets suggested a family in residence. The ferret in his pocket poked a pink nose into the air.

"Try Betsy first," advised Jimmy. "Give 'er a chance to shift 'em."

The children had stayed at the vicarage for a whole month this summer without their parents, who had gone off on a visit to some American cousins. Father wrote often, exhorting them to be good, the boys to help Aunt Maud in the garden, and the girls to make themselves useful to Aunt May with the house-work. "Some hopes," grumbled Lionel; "they'll get the best of it, and I am the only one old enough to wheel a barrow." David at four years old was too miserable most of the time to be of any use at all. The two older girls, Norah and Julia, quite enjoyed helping in the kitchen and pestered Aunt May to be allowed to whisk eggs or lick spoons.

It was therefore a transgression of the first order to be overstaying their time, being late for supper as well as associating with Jimmy, whose clothes smelt so strongly of ferret that it was a wonder that he did not scare every rabbit for miles; moreover, keeping David out past his bed-time, which now seemed utterly unimportant. On this last night of their holiday

Aunt Maud had threatened extensive ablutions for all five, the girls to have their hair washed and put in curlers (except Kathie whose hair curled of its own accord in a wild tossing mane). David was to have his toenails cut, an operation he was determined to resist with all his strength.

There had been no sound from the hole for some time when at last Jimmy said "'Er's stuck."

So there was nothing they could do but wait. Norah and Julia wandered back to the stile into the field and found a few over-ripe blackberries which they ate, staining their fingers and lips and pinafores. Astride a fallen tree David applied himself to the extraction of a colony of woodlice which he picked off into an empty matchbox he had removed from Jimmy's pocket. Kathie squatted by the rabbit hole into which Jimmy continued at intervals to thrust his arm amongst the roots seeking for a grip of Betsy's tail.

Just as Lionel began to say "It's no good, we'll have to get a spade and dig her out," there was a great scuffling and Betsy backed out of the hole. Lionel seized her hind legs and wrenched free a dog so much disguised by earth as to render her brown patches almost indistinguishable from the white. "My gar!" said Jimmy, "We got some bluddy trubble yer!"

Kathie exclaimed in dismay "Oh poor Betsy, poor little dog! – Her eyes are all full of earth! Poor little thing!"

Lionel found a length of cord in a pocket ever bulging with treasures, and tied a noose round the dog's neck.

"I'll lead her," he insisted. "Come on David, leave those beetles."

"Not beetles," defended David stoutly, "they's grammer-sows." He began to wail, and his sisters came hurrying back at the sound.

Betsy submitted with unusual patience to the cleaning opera-tion meted out to her in the stable yard. A dandy brush and curry comb under a stream of water eagerly pumped by Kathie removed most of the mud, but the shivering creature that emerged presented another problem.

"Er's clean enough," said Jimmy, "but 'er's cold – put 'er in be the kitchen fire."

They stared at him. "The kitchen!" gasped Julia, "Aunt Maud would have a fit!"

"She can go into my bedroom," offered Kathie. But Kathie's little room, once Nanny's, opened off a larger nursery bedroom occupied by her sisters, who refused to give asylum to a wet dog still smelling very strongly of rabbit burrow.

"I know a place she can go," went on Kathie, "there's a basket in the attic – "

"But we aren't allowed – " and "How did you get –?"The others stared at her. The attic was out of bounds, said to be Aunt Maud's own special territory and full of stores.

"I went to hide one day," feebly, and then 'No one need know." Lionel considered. Then he said "Well, if we creep up one by one – " They all looked at David, who did not appear to have heard, being absorbed in floating a few remaining woodlice in the trough.

The plan was so simple really. At the kitchen door David was seized by Aunt May and carried off to his bath. "Hurry now, all of you," she called. "You're very late already."

The children hurried up the back stairs with Betsy clasped damply in Lionel's jersey. On the landing they paused, but there was no sound from either Uncle Henry's room or from Aunt Maud.

"I've never been up here before," observed Julia, as the attic door creaked open, revealing strange shapes and mounds in the dim light. "What does Aunt mean by 'stores'?". There seemed to be a lot of old furniture; an ancient hip bath, painted khaki on the outside with a grimy cream lining, held a great pile of old magazines, mostly of an ecclesiastical nature. A parrot's cage long ago vacant was draped with a dirty cotton bedspread, and when Kathie moved a heap of old curtains a cascade of mothballs revealed a woven basket, whose lid completely enclosed its base. It seemed to be quite heavy.

"Let me," said Lionel. "It will make a lovely bed for her. We'll take it down to my bedroom."

The lid stuck a little, and some of the straw binding broke under his fingers. As he prised off the lid there was a strange musty smell from the folded blanket inside.

"Oh!" exclaimed Kathie with delight. "It's a doll!" The blanket drawn back revealed a little bundle tightly wrapped in an old towel, yellow with age. Suddenly she was not sure.

"What is it?" Norah asked. But she knew the answer. "It's a funny sort of a doll – " and then they all drew back from the terrible truth.

"It's a baby," Kathie's face lost all its colour and she sat back, leaning against her sister. "I feel sick," she said.

At half past six each evening Aunt Maud carried a little silver tray into the study, where her brother still pored over his papers. On the tray there was a heavy cut glass decanter of spiced raisin wine and three glasses. Tonight Aunt May was still administering comfort to David, now tucked into bed after his supper of honey-sweetened bread and milk, and happily re-united with his stuffed toys.

The children regarded the study as only a little less holy than the vestry in the church where Uncle Henry robed himself in most gorgeous colours before addressing the small drab group of the faithful. He did not encourage his nieces to visit the study, but Lionel, by virtue of his recent scholarship to a choir school, might take books from the glass-fronted bookcase and peruse with care and clean hands. The books were mostly stuffy old treatises on the history of the church and clergy, but there were also Uncle Henry's school prizes, a copy of *Swiss Family Robinson* in a dark green embossed cover inscribed on the fly-leaf 'Kingswood School, 1862 Prize for Progress – Henry Tregarthen Bray'.

Here too were the aunts' Sunday School prizes: *Stepping Heavenward, or Aunt Jane's Hero*, and *Faithful unto Death*. There was a little book of verse by Aunt Maud entitled *The Snow and Other Poems*. Lionel could not imagine Aunt Maud as a poet. It seemed very poor stuff after *The Fighting Temeraire*.

"Children are late tonight." Henry returned the gold watch on its chain to his pocket after checking it with the mahogany clock on the mantlepiece. Aunt Maud shuffled nervously in her chair. Soon Aunt May could be heard hurrying along the tiled hall, and she had just taken the first sip of wine from her glass when the door was pushed open and the children appeared, closely bunched together.

Lionel began his carefully rehearsed confession.

"I think we ought to tell you," he said steadily, "that we have found a baby in the attic." ("A dead one," put in Kathie, "in a basket.")

"We know we shouldn't have been up there," continued Lionel, "but we were looking for somewhere to hide Betsy; she was so cold and wet that we couldn't leave her in the stable, so we were going to wrap her in a blanket – but Kathie said there was a basket – and that was it," he ended tearfully.

None of the children had been prepared for the scene that followed, nor did they ever forget it. Uncle Henry had put down his glass of wine with great precision upon the inlaid table top and had risen from his chair with a terrible calm. Aunt Maud gave a little gasp that was nearly a sob, and caught Aunt May's shoulders to her hard, flat chest. But Aunt May began to shake and cry hysterically, pushing her away, and her words seemed not to make sense to the now horrified children. Aunt Maud pressed her down into a chair and began to talk harshly and firmly. "Now May, now May – it's all over and forgotten – it's a long time ago and you promised never to think about it. Stop crying now and listen to Maudie."

Uncle Henry's voice cut across the room like a saw. "Maud, tell me."

"Garth dear; dear, dear Garth." No one had heard either of the aunts use his pet name before. "It's over forty years. Let it go now, let her be."

"I must know," Henry insisted, his voice quiet and compelling. Then he saw the children, ashen-faced. "Go to your room, girls, and get ready for bed. Lionel, you stay."

It seemed hours before they heard their brother's bedroom door shut behind him. Almost at once there was a gentle tap on their own door and Uncle Henry's voice courteously requested admission. He stood at the end of the bed for a moment, gripping the black iron with thin fingers.

"I want you to promise me something," he began, "something that must remain a secret for ever. Your aunt is very ill and may not recover from this dreadful shock." Kathie began to cry, but he went on. "I will explain to your parents and they will not question you. I pray you may all forget in time."

"But was it wrong?" asked Norah, "was it so wrong to tell you? I mean – shouldn't it – the baby – be properly buried?"

"Of course." But Uncle Henry's eyes flickered away from her clear blue gaze.

"After all," said Julia thoughtfully, when he had gone, and all three girls were curled up in the big double bed, "we always give the kittens a proper burial."

David was the only cheerful one amongst them when the dogcart arrived in the morning to take their boxes and baskets to the station for the journey home. He was to ride in with Jimmy Lobb, swinging his legs from the padded brown velvet seat, while the girls and Uncle Henry followed in the jingle, driven today for a special treat by Lionel. There had been no sign of Aunt May when they said goodbye to Aunt Maud in the hall, nor did any one of them dare ask for her.

"It's nice to be going home," observed Kathie tactlessly as the pony broke into a brisk trot down the lane. "I hope Betsy is all right."

In the following dogcart Betsy had already shared most of the ginger biscuits given to David to ward off train sickness on the journey. She braced herself comfortably against the rhythm of the trotting pony, her nose as wetly black as liquorice and her white and tan coat gleaming in the sunshine.

Our Day in Luxulyan Woods

Grace Morgan

IT was one of Dad's rare days at home during the summer, and the family were excited at the prospect of going to Luxulyan for a picnic. Away we went in the sunshine.

In those days the green bus stopped just outside our door, and we scrambled upstairs and settled in the front seat. The bus trundled up Tretherys Hill and the sunshine sparkled on the sea below on our left. The china clay boats were waiting to go into Par docks and the seagulls wheeled and screamed overhead, their wings snow-white against the blue sky and sea. At the top of the hill on the left the clay hills too showed up white in the sunshine; when it rains they are a dull grey, but today they looked beautiful. We loved the way the bus wended its way through the narrow lanes and passed the small grey houses, their gardens edged with granite boulders, that made me wish I had some for my own garden. Through Trethurgy village we went, passing the post office and the Men's Institute. There were not many houses then, but now there are a lot of new bungalows.

Eventually we arrived at Luxulyan and left the bus by the old church, where the children always climbed the stone steps outside the graveyard to peep over the wall, a little afraid of the headstones. Everything looked so old. The graveyard sloped down towards a small river and we paused on the ancient bridge to watch the fish, and the dragonflies flitting through the river bushes, their wings transparent and shining. In the spring primroses abound on the banks, and later the bluebells make a blue carpet under the trees stretching for miles. We turned right after leaving the bridge and started into the valley. A small ditch ran along on the right of the roadway. We were very safe from cars and motor bikes; no one came there in those days, and the children could run from side to side, climbing up the small bank on the left where a leat gave a home to larger fish. The water was pure and clean, and there were little open grassy slopes where they lay down in the sunshine, chins almost touching the water, hands trailing along, hoping to catch a fish.

Soon a little white dog joined us, and it led the children along retrieving twigs which they threw into the ditch, when the little dog would bark excitedly for them to do it all over again.

We continued along the valley in warm sunshine until we came to the viaduct which spanned the valley, by which in the old days the horse trains would take the china clay to Ponts Mill to be dried in the clay driers, long low buildings which are still to be seen in the area, used now I think to store timber. The viaduct was a soaring structure with great pillars of granite, and it seemed to reach right up to the sky.

It was cool under the viaduct, where the water rushed over the stones: rounded stones covered with lichen and moss. Under the tall trees windflowers grew, and campion, and the children dug their fingers into the moss and pulled little bits out to take home to make a hanging garden in a basket. There were tiny oak saplings and sycamore shoots, and one wondered what sort of forest they would eventually become.

Soon the children were tired, and we looked for a place to have our picnic. We retraced our steps and descended into an open space littered with huge boulders and beautiful warm stones, where the grass was short and springy. We all sank wearily to the ground and opened the picnic basket. The Cornish pasties had been baked that morning and wrapped in tea cloths, and were hot and full of gravy. Our drink was lemonade made with lemon crystals; there were no bottles of pop in those days; and an apple each rounded off our meal.

Presently the children were full of life again and wanted to do more exploring. Our eldest boy John, who was a lot older than the others, went off on his own to climb up to the viaduct. He was usually very good with the young ones, and we respected his desire to get away for a little while. The young ones went around the huge boulders and we dozed off with our backs against the warm stone. All was peaceful and quiet.

Suddenly I awoke with a sense of dread. The sun seemed menacing and my eyeballs were throbbing. What was wrong? Where were the little ones, I wondered? I staggered to my feet, drowsy with sleep and the hot sun burning down, unable to see, so that all seemed dark. What was happening? I groped my way round the boulders. There was no sound at all, but as my vision cleared I saw the children. Anita was on the edge of a huge pool, looking absolutely terrified, while James our second boy, was about to wade deeper into the water. They were perfectly silent, horror on their little faces. Then I understood.

The boulder, which had seemed so kindly, concealed a deep underground ravine with a strong current. The dog had swum out for a twig and was slowly being sucked under the boulder. Panic stricken, I grabbed James, who in just a few more seconds would certainly have been pulled under the boulder with the poor little dog. Not a word was spoken, the shock to us all going deeper and deeper as the little dog completely disappeared.

We quickly dressed the little ones and hurried to the road.

John joined us at that moment, but no one could explain to him the dreadful happening. We slowly made our way back to the village, and I shuddered as we passed the churchyard, knowing how near we had come to death. As we waited silently for the bus, there were no pleasantries between Dad and some of his colleagues who happened to be there. We crept inside the bus. If the sun was still shining, we were not aware of it, nor of anything, just wanting to get home and be safe inside our four walls and to put the little ones to bed. That evening we sat not speaking, trying to forget the horror: for nights after we would wake in terror of what might have been, thanking God that all was well within the family, but grieving for the unknown little dog.

The Coveted House

Grace Morgan

OLD Sam Agar lived down in the village with his only daughter Mary. His wife had died a few years before. He was a short stocky Cornishman and had spent his working life in the clay quarries. When he finished there he went jobbing gardening, finding digging the earth not so arduous as digging out the clay with huge shovels which could lift a half hundredweight at a time. He had a nasty temper when crossed, and as Mary took after him the villagers would smile and say, "Old Sam's at it again!"

Mary would retire to bed in high dudgeon, but Sam would get out his old bike and take it for a walk up the hill. He never rode the bicycle – but it seemed rather a good idea for an older person to lean on a bike instead of a stick, and it carried his tools.

One of the people for whom he did gardening was an old widow reputed to be 'worth thousands', as she never spent anything and her husband had left her a big house. Rumour had it that she kept five hundred pounds under the bed for an emergency that never came. She was so 'near' that when her poor husband lay dying and his one request was for a small drink of beer, she borrowed an empty beer bottle and put in cold tea – so the poor old man did not get his beer.

Time passed and Sam continued to garden for folks. He was the only one I know who would touch his hat to the gentry!

Suddenly the village was abuzz with the news that Sam was courting again – courting Doris, the woman with the big house. You'd come across the pair under the elder trees and in around the clay dry – a place for drying off the clay in blocks. Mary was furious and said, "It's either her or me." So Sam went and stayed in the big house with Doris. Such a scandal hadn't hit the village for years!

Somehow Mary made him come back. But one day Doris took a taxi round the back of the village to the Registry Office, where he was waiting for her, and they were married. Doris actually bought some new pink knickers – we knew because we saw them on the line a few days later.

Things went quiet for a bit, with Mary simmering down in the village, but then Sam began to get mad with Doris, becoming the master and ordering her about. From being the dominant one in her first marriage she sank to being downtrodden by Sam. Old Sam was at it again, but he did keep the garden well. Then he began to quarrel with the neighbours; and whom should he go to for sympathy? – why his dear Mary of course, down in the village.

Time passed again. Then poor Doris died, and Sam went strutting about, as he was now the new owner of the big house. Being an old-fashioned Cornishman, however, he soon found he needed a woman to wait on him. But Mary refused to have him back. So there was a succession of housekeepers: fat ones, thin ones, jolly ones, and sad ones. No one could stand him for long.

After much advertising a woman arrived from way down west – and from now on Sam became the downtrodden one. She would lock him out in the evenings and he would be taken in by the neighbours. A real sorry old man he became, neglecting the garden. Then the new housekeeper made him sign over the house and money to her. One day the neighbours found him in the garden and he was taken to hospital with a stroke. He died, and now it was Hilda's turn to own the big house.

She had reckoned without Mary, however, who for the first time came to the house and locked Hilda out, throwing her bags out into the lane. And so the villagers never saw Hilda again; but then neither did Mary find the five hundred pounds under the bed.

A few years later there was a police enquiry into Hilda's whereabouts; for it seemed that she made a practice of trying to acquire property from old men. But no one could trace her.

Later still the owners of the quarries up the hill decided to fill in one quarry – called of all things Buggy Pit – with the overburden from the clay hills; and the huge earth removers uncovered poor Hilda's body. And some folks would smile and say, "Old Sam's been at it again." But the reputed five hundred pounds was never unearthed.

After all the strife and argument, and all the talk in the village, the big house became quiet and peaceful; it settled down for the winter knowing that in the spring the flowers would come in the garden, while it waited for new occupants – who perhaps this time would be happier people.

The Legend of Jan Tregeagle

Gordon Harris-Watts

OH that's him, all right. You and I can hear him if we happen to cross Bodmin Moor when the Sun gives the pale Moon right of watch. It's not the howling wind, it's that rogue Tregeagle. For nigh on three hundred years his tortured spirit has fled over the barren moor with the Devil himself and his hounds from Hell in hot pursuit. The Devil laughs as he goads on his hellish pack. He vastly enjoys the chase; he could snatch the frenzied soul in a trice, if he liked, but the Devil is tireless, and enjoys above all things to torture a human soul.

When our children, and theirs, cross the same waste moor, they may still hear Tregeagle's shrill cries of fear and despair flowing in the wind. "No matter," cries the Devil gleefully, "I'll chase him to the end of Time, and then burn him the day after." Harsh treatment, do I hear you say? Not a bit of it. If you'll bear with me, I'll tell you a little of Jan Tregeagle.

'Twas around the year of our Lord 1638, when the good wife of John Tregeagle, Yeoman in the county of Cornwall, living in Bodmin Town, gave birth to their one and only child. The satisfaction of having an heir altered to sorrow and eventually, contempt. "Your son Ma'am, will bring white hairs to us before time!" exclaimed Mr Tregeagle. His good lady bowed her head sorrowfully. It was true that the child had no friends. All the children around his age shunned him, with his painfully thin frame and pale tight-skinned countenance, his mean, thin mouth and his small agate black eyes. None of these features did anything to hide his cruel cunning spirit.

He cared nothing for the pain he caused. He was quick to learn what he needed to learn, and at the age of fourteen his father took him to see an old friend, Mr Pendennis, the attorney, who had offices in the High Street. Pendennis was in no way impressed by the boy's looks, but he was quick to see potential talent in the young Tregeagle's neat writing, and his ready answers to the many questions he asked him. Eventually Pendennis told his friend that he could find some small work for the lad to do in the office. "If he satisfies my clerk Hugh Dymond, then well ... who knows!" he added with a smile. Highly pleased with this, John Tregeagle repaired home to his good wife to impart the news. From the next morning on, Jan Tregeagle made his way daily to Mr Pendennis's office. Grudgingly he had to admit to being pleased with his new job. Besides running errands and keeping the office tidy, he often found that he was able to go down to the courthouse, where it gave him the utmost pleasure to view punishment meted out to the criminals.

Mr Pendennis was soon to find that Jan was more than useful around the office, and as time went on the young Tregeagle was given ledger work because of his neatness. When the time came for the cashier to retire, young Tregeagle was given his responsible work.

Though the lawyer had no suspicion, over many years Tregeagle augmented his wages with the aid of the petty-cash; he was too cunning to take large amounts at one time. As for his private life, he indulged in strong drink and bad company. His escapades around the respectable streets of Bodmin during the hours of darkness were scandalous to say the least, but strange to say, these incidents did not reach the ears of his employer. Mr Pendennis's business did not depart from the ordinary sale contracts of farms, or mortgage contracts, the swearing of papers and probate work, so the usual business office routine presented little problem to Jan. Pendennis was highly satisfied with his apparently trustworthy cashier. During these years of young Tregeagle's progress, his father John Tregeagle fell sick and died. This caused no distress to Jan Tregeagle, who at once took possession of the family house. Immediately his poor mother became a drudge, for the serving wench and cook were dismissed out of hand.

Then certain events occurred which were to alter Tregeagle's life completely. There had been a great uprising against the throne of England. The Duke of Monmouth, pretender to the throne, had gathered a great army of followers to his cause. Yeomen and labourers on the farms and many vagabonds joined the rabble, for rabble it was. Few had arms of any kind, fewer knew how to use them, and none knew the inevitability of the carnage that was to follow.

The attempt to overthrow the King was a miserable failure, and the blood of hundreds was poured shamefully into their native soil. Of the undisciplined rabble under Monmouth's standard, those that escaped the sword fled to their homes to hide. Then came a terrible revenge . . . The Lord Chief Justice of England, Judge Jeffreys, took the Western circuit. Here was punishment indeed. The King's highest administrator of justice was a monster in human form. His courts were a mockery of judicature, his inhumanity notorious throughout the kingdom. Feared by all, none was safe from his moods save only the King himself. Wherever he travelled he left a trail of blood, more often than not of innocent blood. There was seldom a punishment other than death from the Hanging Judge. Thus it was that he arrived with heavy escort at Bodmin Town. The whole population of the area trembled at the sight and the thought. The year was 1685 when the Lord Chief Justice prepared to sit and preside over the court.

Jan Tregeagle was fascinated by the event and its certain repercussions. Here was a great man, he thought, a man larger than life. Each day that the court was in session Tregeagle joined the morbid throng who filled the rough benches of the courtroom. He relished the awesome powers that evil judge possessed, and thrilled at the momentary witticisms that the Chief Justice mouthed aside to his cronies, who laughed uproariously, only to cringe abashed and terrified when the judge changed his mood, and thundered out obscene threats instead. His bloated features that smiled at the applause would be transformed by a passion fearful to see. God help the hapless prisoner then in the dock, for he would receive the full force and penalty of Judge Jeffreys' anger!

Then came a day when Tregeagle hatched an evil and dastardly plan. He excused himself early from the office and sought an audience with the awful Judge. He requested to see him in order to give him valuable information concerning certain people in high places who were in sympathy with the rebellion. He was roughly bundled into a small antechamber to await the Judge's pleasure. Now a fit of uncontrollable fear assailed him, warring with the greed that had brought him here. Suddenly the door was swung open and two men-at-arms indicated that he was to follow them. Within a few moments he was ushered into another chamber, and there, sitting at a large table strewn with documents and not a few bottles, was the fearsome figure of Judge Jeffreys. There was a silence during which the judge's baleful and inflamed eyes were fixed on the trembling little figure standing in front of him. Even the men-at-arms, standing in the doorway, shook as though with the palsy when the judge bellowed in a stentorian roar: "Well? . . . Come along varlet, out with it, whatever it is! It had better be something, mind . . .or you'll rue the day!"

Tregeagle was nearly overcome by fright, but managed to bleat out in a falsetto whine, "If it please your Worship, Sire, I accuse my master Richard Pendennis, Lawyer of this town of Bodmin, and his wife, of being actively engaged in treasonable work against our sovereign Lord the King."

"Aha, I know your sort," thundered Jeffreys. "Look at you spindle-legged, wizened crawling slimy thing . . . a Judas eh?" – He turned to the men-at-arms – "Out to curry favour, eh? I'll make it hot for him!" Then in a flash his face was as stone. "Speak up, knave. Your looks remind me of a chicken that desecrated my table yesterday. Come, out with your accusations and be damned for it."

Tregeagle trembled, as well he might, but he repeated his story: "May it please your Worship, my master is a friend of Monmouth."

The Judge smiled a hard smile: "Stands in your way, does he? – No matter, I get more gallows fodder from sly tongues like yours than I can hope for from the witless rabble around me." He reached for his quill pen and wrote a few words – words that sounded a death sentence on the two worthy innocent Pendennises.

It was fated, however, that they should not face a mock trial and shameful death. News came to the childless lawyer from a friend that his evil clerk had borne false witness against him, and that a sentence of death upon him and his kin was already on its way to his home. The lawyer, knowing full well the tortures that would surely come to both him and his wife before the hangman had his way, went in haste to visit his lifelong friend the apothecary, from whom he obtained laudanum, sufficient to ensure a speedy escape from the torments threatening himself and his beloved wife.

Tregeagle had hoped to take up at once the reins of his master's business, but it was not yet to be. The bloody Judge sent for him, and reading his thoughts like a book, rasped, "Not yet, Judas. You'll do a deal more before you earn that reward . . . Nothing do you get . . . until you prise out more maggots from under the corpse of this rebellion. I serve the King, but you'll serve only the Lord Chief Justice of England . . . Get out . . . 'Tis almost on my tongue to send you post haste to the gallows yourself . . . so out, out!"

Tregeagle fled with alacrity from that terrible presence. He at once began to cast about to find victims for Jeffreys to sentence; all had to be innocent victims, for Tregeagle knew none who had been active against the King. First he gave the names of any who might have scorned him, or avoided his company, and then at the cast of a hat, the name of the first person he encountered. Scores of people from one village or another, from one town or another, were marked out for death in order to provide fit entertainment for the Hanging Judge.

On the last day of the Bodmin assizes Judge Jeffreys sent for Tregeagle. He regarded the now hardened villian with a sneer. "I do believe I've made you a thorough rogue by now, a rogue ready to meet your true master." He poured out two large tankards of strong drink. "Drink," he commanded. Tregeagle gasped and spluttered as the fiery spirit burned down his throat. Jeffreys drank his in the manner of the hardened drunkard, and again, as the tankards were replenished, he forced Tregeagle to do likewise. Then, his eyes burning into Tregeagle's very soul, he said: "Now my fine Judas, wouldst meet thy true master?"

Tregeagle trembled violently, not knowing what to expect. "I'm not worthy my lord!"

"No matter," roared Jeffreys, "you'll meet him soon enough, I'll warrant."

It was then arranged that Tregeagle should be assigned to the rank of magistrate and assume ownership of all the Pendennis property, while Judge Jeffreys returned to London town. There, his reign came to a terrible end. He was sent to The Tower, whence an attempted escape in disguise brought him death by his own foul hand.

Meanwhile Tregeagle's life became ever more malignant. None was safe from his powers. He held court, dealing out a devious justice, designed to enhance his own power and riches. His judgements were a mockery, many good farmers losing their lands and being turned from their homesteads. Many died from want and exposure in the winters that followed. All this must be laid at the door of Tregeagle. He was as much a servant of the Devil as Judge Jeffreys; his powers to deal extreme penalties were not as great, but his evil will was ever there.

Then came a crime that he contemplated with a deal of pleasure, which was to marry a young maiden of high estate, the wealthy family of Tihidy Manor, the Polgreens. Trelawney Polgreen had wrested a fortune from the bowels of the Cornish rock, for tin was a metal of great price, and many years of mining had added wealth to the Polgreens' position among the landed gentry of the Duchy.

Tregeagle planned to kill two birds with one stone, and first, to woo the daughter.

To say that Tregeagle was presentable to the young lady would be a travesty. His appearance had nothing to recommend it; his thin legs now had to carry, not the scraggy body of his youth, but one bloated by excesses licensed by his ill-gotten wealth. His mean countenance, once sallow, was now disfigured by the many red veins in his cheeks; his nose was swollen, red and pimpled by heavy eating and drinking; his eyes even more cruel than his thin slit of a mouth. No; Jan Tregeagle's evil smelled in company.

Tregeagle's ambition to possess Trelawney Polgreen's fair daughter kept him awake at night. But this was not the only thing to disturb his slumbers, for Tregeagle had hardly had a night free from the constant vision of the fiery eyes of the now departed Judge Jeffreys. Those glowing orbs that in life had paralysed Tregeagle with fear had lost not one whit of their evil power in death.

At some time during the life of the good Mr Pendennis, Mr Polgreen had done some business with him. Tregeagle found this an adequate excuse to call on the gentleman at the manor house. Mr Polgreen had an heir, Rufus Polgreen, a son of twenty one years, a fine upstanding young man. His daughter Rachel was now just turned sixteen years, as pretty a maiden as could be seen for miles around. Mrs Polgreen was, like her good husband, plump and pleasant. This was the family that Jan Tregeagle had met that fateful day, coming among them like plague, or a wolf in sheep's clothing.

At first it appeared, even to Tregeagle, that his desires relating to the young Rachel were doomed . . . unless he could weave some plot that would entangle the girl. In his frustration he became morose and unapproachable at his office, though he still drew some pleasure from his days at court.

It occurred to him to search for a weakness with Mr Polgreen, and he found that the old gentleman loved playing at cards, though merely for pleasure. How could Tregeagle turn this to his advantage? Then came a certain night when he was sitting in bed, racking his brains for a plan to involve the old gentleman. Suddenly a great red glow of light, as of a roaring fire in the grate, appeared at the foot of his bed. Startled, Tregeagle shrank back against the bedhead. Then with a noise as of steam from a hot spring, a figure appeared; and such a figure! Tregeagle swooned; as he came round he heard the Lord Chief Justice Jeffreys calling to him: "Varlet, Judas, meet with your true master!" But Tregeagle saw that it was not the judge that stood at the foot of the bed . . . no . . . it was the Devil himself! As Tregeagle gazed at this apparition, through his terror he heard his mean little soul call to his inner thoughts: 'Serve this master as you served Jeffreys, and you'll be looked after, better than you ever have been before!'

Greed gave Tregeagle courage, and emboldened to parley with the Evil One, he soon made a contract with him.

Tregeagle was to have the Devil's aid to possess Rachel Polgreen and the estates and mansion house of Trelawney Polgreen, in exchange for which the Devil required of Tregeagle his soul. Each partner fancied that he had got the better bargain.

It now became strangely easy for Tregeagle to persuade Polgreen to play cards for money. Having once begun, night after night they played, and night after night the old gentleman lost heavily. Though Tregeagle had little skill, the Devil put

winning cards in his hand. The gambling reached a point when
Mrs Polgreen pleaded to the son Rufus to induce his father to
cease this senseless gambling. One night the son watched as
Tregeagle and Polgreen duelled, the old man always losing and
ever increasing his stakes for the next game. Rufus watched for
trickery on Tregeagle's part, and he could find none. But late in
the evening the Devil, who was ever in attendance, and who
really dealt the cards, held one trump card too long in his own
fiery hand. The card suddenly glowed red and burst into flames.

Rufus, though he could see no explanation for this extra-
ordinary phenomenon, was sure that his father was being
cheated. He challenged Tregeagle, and drew his sword.
Tregeagle was terrified; he knew nothing of duelling and wore
his sword only for ornament – but with a chuckle the Devil
stood in front of Tregeagle and crossed swords with Rufus.
Although Rufus saw only Tregeagle it was the Devil who calmly
thrust his sword through poor Rufus's heart and laid the son
dead at his frantic father's feet. The anguish of the sorrowing
parents was terrible to see. In the midst of the mother's
lamentation Tregeagle only smiled.

After the mourning had run its course, Polgreen pondered
over his great financial losses to Tregeagle, and then quietly he
met him at a secret place and agreed to play once more, in the
hope of regaining his fortune.

This is what Tregeagle wanted, for the Devil had told him to
be a little easy on the old man at first, and then . . . "We'll take
all from him!" That same night Tregeagle and Polgreen met to
play. Polgreen, determined to regain his lost money, gambled
rashly. With the Devil silently goading him on, the old man
staked his entire estate, mansion and farms, every stick and
stone. He lost. Beside himself with grief and despair, the Devil
put one last thought into his tottering brain: 'Wager the hand of
your only daughter against everything that Tregeagle possesses
. . . you must win in the end!' The old man thought wildly 'I'll
do it . . . I'll win this time; see if I don't!'

"My daughter's hand against your fortune, Tregeagle . . . and
the money you've already won from me . . . and may the Lord
have mercy on my soul!" Polgreen said these words with so
much conviction that even the Devil recoiled, while Tregeagle,

quickly recovering, sneered to himself: 'The old man isn't going to get any help from that quarter; he's being too greedy!'

The last hand was dealt; and how could it go otherwise than for Tregeagle to know that he had the daughter's hand as well as the old man's property?

As the delighted rogue turned to explain to Polgreen that he must sign a deed to confirm his vow, Polgreen's poor heart stopped beating and he fell to the floor.

Tregeagle was baffled, for he saw everything that he had gambled for snatched from him.

But still the Devil appeared to be on his side. "Quickly," he cried, "pick him up, put him in the chair. Now get the quill-pen."

Tregeagle obeyed instantly. He took the pen to the dead man's hand. "He can't sign this paper; he's dead!"

The Devil looked around the dimly lit room. In a flash his hand seized a large fly that was lazily hovering around the candles, and in a trice he thrust the living fly into the old man's open mouth. Holding his hand there to cover the mouth, he said to Tregeagle: "Put the pen in his hand and guide it to write his signature. While there's life in a body, a witnessed stroke of the pen is legal."

Tregeagle did as he was told, and Polgreen's name appeared, roughly legible, on the fateful document.

"I'll bear witness," roared the Devil, and he scored his name on the signed paper.

Tregeagle then left the house, leaving the body to be found by the servants later. The day after Polgreen's funeral, Tregeagle returned, to take possession of both the daughter and the manor house. On hearing his demands, Mrs Polgreen had a seizure, and collapsed. Rachel, on being shown the document and believing the foul thing to be true and therefore valid, rushed to her rooms, stabbed herself with a pair of scissors, and died. Tregeagle, thinking he was on the point of victory, allowed himself to be taken by the enraged servants. But all he got from the Devil, instead of protection, was a laugh and a quiet – "I've kept my part of the bargain. Be sure you haven't seen the last of me." That was reassurance to Tregeagle.

The appalling violence to such a prominent family in Cornwall at once brought Tregeagle in front of high administrators of the

Law. At the hearing the court was crowded with the numerous victims of Tregeagle's many other swindles and forgeries. Knowing all were against him, when the fatal document with the forged signature of Polgreen was brought for evidence Tregeagle cried out "I am innocent; this signature is not false; I have my witness . . . the Devil himself !"

The court was aghast: "We cannot have such blasphemy here!" But in a flash of thunder and acrid blue smoke, there stood the Evil One himself. Pandemonium broke out, as people screamed and fainted.

The Devil laughed as his hot hands singed black the oaken witness box. "Come, ye miserable so-called purveyors of Justice and Right, hearken to me," he roared out. He pointed a long finger at Tregeagle. "The wretch before you on trial is guilty of all the crimes brought against him now and many more that you know not of . . . Hurry, I say . . . Find the varlet guilty . . . and then I'll have his paltry soul!"

At these words he vanished, leaving the courtroom in uproar, the appearance of the Devil having proved too much for all but the bravest or most foolhardy. With difficulty the judge gathered his strength and in a shaking treble murmured, "We find Jan Tregeagle guilty of all the charges brought against him." He went on to pronounce the death penalty, at which the Devil reappeared. Laughing with hideous glee he plunged his burning hand right down the gullet of Tregeagle, and drew out his soiled soul. Tregeagle's lifeless body dropped to the floor. With a shrill unearthly scream the soul, a pale shadow of his earthly appearance, wriggled out of the Devil's grasp, and fled headlong out of the courtroom. The Devil gave a great roar of demonic laughter, and set off in pursuit. Panic by now had broken out, and there was a mad terrified rush by all to the doors. In a few moments the courtroom was empty, and there for several days Tregeagle's body lay untouched, until a few brave souls ventured to move it to unconsecrated ground.

From that day on, and for ever, the spindle-legged form of Tregeagle scampers over gorse and rock, screaming and howling with terror . . . and close behind follows the Devil and his hounds of hell. And so the chase will go on, until the day of Kingdom Come.

The Workhouse Key

Gordon Harris-Watts

AFTER many doubts about our new adventure, now that we had made the flight from Pretoria to London's Heathrow we both felt in more optimistic mood. Emma was looking radiant, her Titian hair swinging with every move of her head and an infectious glint in her hazel eyes. "I can't wait to see this Cornwall of your ancestors," she confided.

My great grandfather had been born in Cornwall, near Penzance, around the year 1860. After working in the English Post Office, he decided to seek his fortune in South Africa; evidently he was good at his job, for he rose to the position of Post Master General in Johannesburg. My father sought his living in the wine trade out there. He prospered, and in time came to own a small wine business. When I left college I joined him and by the age of twenty-five I was a junior executive. I married Emma twelve months later, and it was decided that I should come to England. The company was planning to expand the business just at the time that a certain old-established wine and spirit business had been advertised in the trade journal; it was situated in Penzance, Cornwall. My father, proud of his Cornish blood, thought it a good omen, so after the usual preliminaries it was purchased, and my fate was decided. I liked the idea, mind you, and so did Emma, although we had never been out of South Africa before. Emma was three years younger than I and from the same district, where we had been at school together.

We spent little time in London as I had made reservations at a recommended hotel in Penzance and within forty-eight hours we were again on the move, this time to our new life. On the trip down by rail Emma and I were fascinated by the wide variety of scenery over such a small distance. Eventually we drew near to Cornwall; the sight of the famous Brunel bridge evoked many of the tales that my father had heard from his grandfather which I now retold, while Emma sat opposite me, hands folded in her lap. Some of the tales she had heard from me before, but now we were almost in that land of legend they were taking on another dimension. A book I had picked up at Paddington Station contained a map of the West Country and I pointed out how the river Tamar almost severed the county from the mainland. According to legend, this physical feature was brought about by an awesome task set by the Gods: they commanded three giants to carve through the granite moors, and thereby free the land of mists from Britain forever. The giants toiled ceaselessly, the springs eagerly filling in the great chasms, until after many lifetimes of ordinary man, within sight of completion of their terrible labours, they all fell exhausted, and died. Whatever the legend or the scientist says, the Tamar almost allows Cornwall to be termed an island. While I talked, and Emma listened, we approached and crossed the wrought-iron masterpiece. The miles passed under the wheels of our train, Emma drowsed and I allowed my mind to be carried into fantasy. The very air promised things, many secrets still untold.

Arriving at Penzance, we were quickly in our hotel room and then when we had had a hearty meal Emma was eager to explore the town. There was a whiff in the air of the sea, and the September afternoon was bright, even passably warm. The streets were quaint with narrow pavements, some elevated and reached by steps, and everywhere the lovely burr of the Cornish tongue and rosy faces wreathed with merry smiles, as though the general opinion was:"We'm Carnish, and proud of it". The promenade had a fascinating blend of ozone, fish, and tar; Emma and I breathed in vast amounts of the magical brew. I wondered what awesome effect such a combination would have if introduced to some of the French perfume houses.

Of course, one point of prime interest was my new headquarters, the first British branch of South Africa Wine. We quickly found the building, which still bore the name of the old business, and we stood looking at the Georgian frontage.

"Harry, it's beautiful."

I agreed with pardonable pride, so eager was I to start my new venture.

The next day being Sunday, we took advantage of another mild day to make ourselves fairly familiar with the layout of the little town.

Emma spotted a street with two or three estate agencies. "I'll look around those tomorrow, Harry; we shall have to get our own place. I don't want to stay at a hotel longer than necessary."

I agreed. "You get some brochures, dear, and when I get back from the office, we can browse through them.

The day we had been waiting for arrived. I was up early, breakfasted, and took my leave of Emma, who was longing to go shopping.

I arrived at my new offices at nine to meet the staff who were already there, for we had arranged to keep on those of the original employees who wanted to stay. There was perhaps a little tension in the air, but I did my best to explain to them that all I wanted was their co-operation, with the same standard of service that they had given to their previous employer. I decided to open a couple of bottles of our own wine, and we all then toasted the success of the new business. That was soon over, and the air somewhat cleared. It was soon apparent that Mrs Fowler, the private secretary who had served the previous owner for several years, a woman of about forty, was very efficient. This was a great relief to me; good secretaries are scarce. Both she and Mr Buss, the senior member of the staff, were invaluable in the operation of re-organisation.

That first morning session was so absorbing that I lost sight of time, until Mrs Fowler tactfully suggested that it was the hour for lunch. The end of the working day came to a satisfactory conclusion and I arrived back at our hotel tired, but feeling pleased with the world.

Emma had been busy visiting estate agents and showered me with particulars of all sorts of properties. "Darling, just look at some of these; the agents are so polite and helpful, very eager to help us buy a place."

"I'll bet they are," I laughed.

At our table at dinner Emma chatted endlessly about the shops, the people, and of course, the houses.

Glancing at the backs of some of the lists, I whistled at the figures. "Some of these prices are a bit naughty, aren't they?"

Emma pouted. "You must make allowances; you are in England now, dear."

There was little I could say to that. "Look dear, why don't

you come along to the office tomorrow around lunch time? I'll leave a bit early and we can go to one or two of these agents."

The weather was still pretty good; not what we had been used to in South Africa, but at any rate dry. Emma arrived as arranged, and I was pleased to introduce her to Mr Buss and Mrs Fowler. I sat on the end of my desk and surveyed Emma. "You look a thousand dollars; where have you been shopping? And how much have you put me in the red?" Still, when we left the office I was proud of the figure she cut, as we weaved through the jostling shoppers.

Emma came to a halt outside an impressive property office, where many photographs of various fine looking properties were on view in the windows. This was our first call. A youthful attendant, no doubt impressed by the vision of Emma, retired into an inner sanctum and returned with an older chap, the agent himself.

He came forward to the counter, a professional smile tied to his countenance. "Can I help you?" – This was certainly not a Cornish voice.

Emma didn't give me a chance to start our inquiry. "We would like to see some of your properties."

The agent invited us to a couple of comfortable leather armchairs and drew up another for himself. "And what sort of price limit would you be thinking of? Could I take your name? – Just for our record, you know." His closer proximity gave us the benefit of a much advertised after-shave. He waited hopefully for Emma and me to name our ideas of price tags.

I told him our price limit and he asked the younger man to bring the B file. This was brought to him, and with the dexterity of a member of the Magic Circle he shuffled and searched, until we had a sizable batch of particulars in front of us.

I looked at the agent, who coincidentally answered to the name of Home. "Let me put you in the picture as to what we desire. We don't want a dolled up modern property, nor do we want a fourteen bedroomed manor house." Emma laughed.

He was a trifle disconcerted for a second and then once again resumed his flow: "I understand of course, Mr King. I should be more than delighted to personally escort you to one or two properties that come to mind."

I looked at the time. "I could spare an hour, if that's enough."

"That will be fine, if you would like to come along to the car." He was on his feet in a flash, and ushering us out to a very new Jaguar.

We had been going about ten minutes when he turned off the main road: "We have a fine property just along here, only just on our books; a real gem."

He passed the particulars of the property over to Emma, and I glanced over her shoulder. "Oh, The Old Workhouse; that's unusual."

The agent looked sharply back at me, his eyes behind his thick pebble glasses puzzled. He took the particulars back; looking at them, his face cleared. "You had me puzzled for a moment Mr King; I thought you said The Old Workhouse. This is Manor Cottage."

Emma glanced at me queerly.

"What made you make a mistake like that, Harold?"

I was mystified myself, for I was sure that I had seen the title on the paper and I was certain I had not heard the name before. At that moment we slowed down and got out at the entrance of Manor Cottage. How could I have made such a blunder, I wondered. I felt a bit of a fool. Of course, photographs of properties for sale are generally second-rate, but to conjure up a name such as I did was odd. But the agent and Emma had apparently forgotten all about it.

Manor Cottage had no appeal for me, and Emma was obviously not impressed. When the agent had unlocked the door Emma stood in the passage inside and eyed the immediate surroundings.

"No," she pronounced, "this is definitely not us." She shuddered. "It's claustrophobic."

I am usually not so forthright in my opinions, but I agreed with Emma. "No," I said, "the windows are too small; the place would cost a mint to bring to what I would call comfort."

The agent was not unduly abashed. I could see he was disappointed, but with the zeal of a true salesman, he delved into his brief-case and produced another illustrated folder. "Have a look at this one Mr King; another fine bargain, not ten minutes from here."

I took the proffered folder. There in black and white was a

hazy picture of a long low stone building and a not too distinct heading, The Old Workhouse. "Ha, this is it, The Old Workhouse; I must have seen this one before. The catalogues must have got mixed up; yes, I like the look of it." I handed it to Emma.

The agent stared at me; in a strange sort of way he seemed a trifle upset. "Mr King, I don't understand; you are looking at the details of The Barn, one of our nicest properties, modernised at great expense two years ago.

Impatiently now, I took the papers from Emma, who appeared visibly uncomfortable, and pushed them into the hands of the agent. "Here, this is it, plain enough."

"Mr King, let me assure you, we have no such property on our books."

Emma tugged my jacket. "Whatever has come over you, Harold?" Her eyes showed her concern. "I think we had better go back now; you've been worrying too much about the business." She turned to the mystified agent. "You know we have only just arrived from South Africa, and Harold has been very busy, opening the new branch."

"I understand, Mrs King." He looked across at me. "You probably have been burning the midnight oil, as it were, I . . . er . . ."

I had really made a fool of myself, and God alone knew why or how this blessed workhouse complex had come into my brain.

The agent smiled a weak smile. "The peculiar thing is that we have never had such a named property on our books." Actually, he looked as though he was glad he hadn't.

I turned to Emma, who seemed torn between the emotions of concern for me and embarrassment for both of us. He smiled politely, even bravely, considering my strange conduct. This persistent illusion of mine was worrying me, too: why should I imagine seeing a place that didn't exist? Rather shamefacedly Emma and I got into the agent's car and without another word he started up, and drove us back to Penzance. By this time he had apparently regained his poise. "Perhaps when you are ready, you will do me the honour of viewing some of our other properties; I'm sure that we will find your ideal home."

We muttered some pleasantries, and left him. I don't know

when I remember feeling such a buffoon; I could have kicked myself, while Emma was concerned about my mental well being.

"Are you feeling all right in yourself, dear?"

"Look love, what I said I saw, I saw. I can't give you any logical reason or explanation; I'm as mystified as you. But each time he showed me a blessed brochure, there was this damn workhouse."

I will say this for Emma, she can quickly put unpleasant things out of her mind. To her it is all part of her design in life, of being a good wife to me. I had to get back to the business, while Emma thought the pleasure of a bit of shopping might take her mind off the unsuccessful morning.

Another week passed quickly. I was absorbed in my job and Emma was determined to find an agent with the right property, and so I heard about little else when I got home. No doubt this living in limbo, with no real home of our own, was getting us both on edge. We went to another agent, Watson and Partners – very good people, I was told – who showed us several properties, but damn it ... that workhouse title sat directly over anything they produced. I realised now how serious this was. Had I picked up some bug – perhaps some malady of the eyes, or stomach? – I brooded over it quite a lot and Emma found that I was much preoccupied.

"You are going to see a doctor, Harold; we have to sign on with one of them, anyway. I inquired at the office and Mr Buss recommended a Dr Budd. I've phoned his surgery, and fixed an appointment."

Emma went to the surgery with me and waited for me while I spoke to the doctor. He was a decent sort, a Rugby fanatic, and when I mentioned that I was South African, I thought he would never stop talking about that sport. Once we got to the reason for my visit he became serious. He gave me a thorough check-up, then spoke of mental strain. I said that our only trouble at the moment was that we were anxious to install ourselves in a home of our own. He seized on that like a dog on a bone. "There's your trouble, Mr King. I'll give you a tonic, and do come along in a day or two. Nothing to worry about really you know; mountains out of molehills you know." He laughed cheerily.

"All right for you!" I thought. I came out to Emma, who looked strained. "It's all right dear; not to worry". As we walked to the chemist with the prescription the doctor had given me we agreed to let the whole thing be forgotten. We decided that the illusion must have come from some long forgotten incident, and something had triggered off some sort of mental mirage.

The next three or four months were tabulated in my desk diary; the pages showed business progress and staff efficiency, but sometimes domestic frustrations clouded the otherwise satisfactory reading. Emma and I had moved out of the hotel and taken a furnished flat near the town centre. We still were unable to find the house that would become our very own home, but I dreaded the idea of going through the previous ordeal again. Emma took it on herself to visit the various estate agents; she knew I trusted her logical mind, and what would give her happiness and content would surely meet with no opposition from me. Without saying anything to Emma I glanced through a small batch of illustrated folders she had left on a coffee table. To my intense horror, I no sooner surveyed each picture than that vague, misty, long, low building sprang to my eyes, with the heading – 'The Old Workhouse'. I resolved then and there, that I would find some excuse to be absent or too busy, when Emma came to take me home-shopping.

It was during this period that I developed an interest in my ancestry. I went to the local library to borrow some books on the subject. I hadn't realised until then the importance of the church register, or the local registrar. Emma and I decided to have lunch together and call at the registrar's office in Penzance. The weather was still quite pleasant and the holiday crowds had long left the town to the locals but life was becoming a trifle tedious, as far as Emma was concerned. Our inability to find a place of our own was frustrating to both of us, but Emma was a home type and was missing our small bungalow way back home.

We found that the registrar was a pleasant lady, who also acted as private secretary to one of the town's solicitors. She willingly searched through her records, but she had to admit defeat. "I'm sorry Mr King, but there doesn't seem to be any record of members of your family. Of course, there are always the church registers." She turned away, to put some papers back into the cabinet, and then said, "If you have the time to spare, Mr King, there is a regular bus service that leaves the square every hour. It serves a number of small outlying hamlets and villages. I would suggest that you both take a trip; it's bound to be something different for you both, and who knows? You may even find the very church that your ancestors attended."

We took our leave, thanking her for her kind help. The day was a fine one, and we decided to take the bus, just to see where it would take us. It was almost ready to start, so taking two returns, and making sure of returning times, we settled ourselves into a rather hard seat. The bus started off with a full load of which Emma and I were obviously the only non-Cornish passengers; here we were among the real country folk. We sat enchanted by the whole scene: the soft burr of the 'Carnish' dialect and the lovely green backcloth of trees and grass, a green that one only finds in Britain. The first stop was announced by the conductor, whose words sounded like "Yers Gulval, me dears." A couple of elderly ladies alighted leisurely, helped by the conductor.

Emma tugged at my arm. "Let's get out here, Harold".

I would have been loth to have passed that village without looking at it properly, so we got out, not before making sure that the bus would pick us up on the return. As it drew away Emma and I walked hand in hand toward the village centre. Nestled among aged oak and ash, stood a gem in granite. The urge that had motivated generations of worshippers, caused us to move into the churchyard. One could imagine this ancient pile of granite as a lodestone, surrounding itself with crops of various less imposing stone, each single one calling out to the living: "Standing or fallen I cover and mark one who did worship and pray in that granite house of God." Even the ordinary sounds of the village seemed to recede as we approached the entrance. The great double oak doors were open. Such weak sunshine as there was only magnified the gloom beyond those doors. We hesitated just for a brief moment, and then a figure emerged from the dim interior, it seemed a vast figure, garbed in unmistakable dog collar and cassock – the Vicar. He smiled and greeted us gently; we answered formally and I introduced Emma and myself as newcomers to Cornwall "We are very interested in the area, Father. My ancestors came from this part of Cornwall, and I am very keen to trace their actual birthplace." He took an immediate interest: "Well, well, we must do what we can to assist. My name, by the way, is Norman Sharp; I have been in this parish these twenty years now; still an emmet to some, though." He laughed a vast belly laugh. I am not a tall man, and I was already tiring of looking up at this giant of a man. He waved us into the church. "We are very proud of our little church, dating from the fifteenth century." His voice boomed through the empty building, receiving an immediate endorsement from the echoing chasm. Again, I took umbrage at his heartiness; I've always found that most people tend to speak in hushed voices in such surroundings; still, I supposed the Vicar had grown immune to the atmosphere.

Emma and I followed him into the vestry, where he passed his hand across several old church registers: "Ha, now let's look in this one: you say your great-grandfather must have been born about – " and he looked inquiringly down at me. I had that more or less worked out. "Well Vicar, I would reckon that he must have been born around 1850 or 1860." The Vicar expertly turned over several pages, pausing now and again, when he saw a name that looked like King. Then he burst out in triumph: "My dear Mr King, you really are in luck. Here we have a record of marriage, not very legible mind you, but indisputably, yes, Samuel King, Bachelor, to Elizabeth Gwent, Spinster. 1851, on September 13th. Now we seem to be in the hunt." He was obviously enjoying this. "Ha, yes, here we have a first born, a son. Harold King, born 1852. This is what you were looking for, Mr King; this would appear to be a record of the birth of your great-grandfather. Well, well! You are very fortunate to have ventured into Gulwal – astonishingly so, really." He was quite excited. I agreed with him; truly I had not known that this was the home of my ancestors. But the Vicar hadn't finished yet. "Here we are again; another child of the marriage, a daughter this time, and christened in this church as . . . Florence King, in the year 1856, May the . . . er . . .I don't seem to . . . oh yes, it's the 15th. The ink has faded badly." He scanned further pages.

"No more, I'm afraid. A pity." He looked disappointed, as though two offspring were not enough. However, we had achieved more than I had dared hope for. I was delighted, for I had no idea that the former Postmaster General of Johannesburg ever had a sister. I felt that I had to show my appreciation somehow. There was an offertory box in the aisle. Emma went over and put something in it, and I took out my wallet and extracted a fiver – I regarded the information that I had received as well worth it.

Our business completed, we wended our way to the entrance. It really was a lovely old church, well worth the visit on its own account. Standing for a moment at the doorway, we blinked in the outer light, weak though it was. "Such a great pleasure to have met you both; I trust we shall soon have the pleasure of seeing you again." With a gracious smile, the Vicar held out a huge hand: I almost shuddered at the idea of having my normal size hand crushed, but I need not have worried; those banana-sized digits had about as much gripping power as a wet fish.

Suddenly, as he was about to turn away from us, I blurted out on an impulse of the moment: "Just one thing, Father. Have you an old workhouse in the village?"

The Vicar smiled tolerantly. "I understand – you desire a little more local history. Yes, there was a small workhouse in this parish – I am thankful such means of providing succour and security are long gone from our midst."

My heart was pumping fast and I felt Emma's small hand suddenly clutch at mine.

He went on. "Yes, the building still stands, now a private dwelling".

Tension mounted inside me. There could be no reason for this, I thought, yet . . . Suddenly it was as if Emma and I were standing in a confessional, with the good Vicar as our mentor.

"Pardon me, Father, if I seem to be rambling off at a tangent, but I had to ask about the workhouse because I have been experiencing a definite fixation: my wife and I have been searching for a house, and each time I am shown the picture of some property, the real picture vanishes, and in its stead, is a phantom house, a mirage that only troubles me when I get hold of one of the leaflets from the estate agent." I almost sighed with relief at that silly confession.

The Vicar gazed at me intently, his dark eyes searching my soul. "Very strange, Mr King, and apparently you have had no reason to image such an out-of-the-ordinary place?"

I spread my arms as I replied "None whatever, sir. The building which appears to me each time is not a clear picture, but then again, what photograph ever appears clear on a property leaflet?"

The Vicar smiled wryly. "Yes, I see your point. Look, why don't you good folk come over to the vicarage with me for a cup of tea?"

I mentally worked out the time at our disposal, nodded to Emma, and accepted the invitation gladly.

The vicarage was adjacent to the church, a rather neglected regency property. When inside the house, the Vicar invited us to make ourselves comfortable while he rustled up some tea and biscuits. Apparently he was on his own. He kept up a constant chatter, mostly to Emma as he sought to bring the conversation back to normalities.

"Now," he started, when we were all with a cup in our hands. "Where were we? Oh yes. Yours is a very strange story, yet I have heard as strange . . . and true." His eyes were bright for a man of his age, and he used them to great effect as he continued, "I would not be of this cloth, if I scoffed at your illusion. Life is such a great mystery in itself" – his voice had softened, deeper now, and grave. "Do you see this image at any other time? Or could you describe the place you see?"

He listened intently to my answers, his face serious. I tried to make light of the whole thing: "What worried me a bit was that my wife never saw the image . . . I felt I must be going mad." I had a grin on my face, but really there was no merriment in my mind.

The Vicar came over to Emma and me, and taking our cups, turned away from us to put them on a side table. When he faced us again – for he spoke with little of his previous gusto – he must have made up his mind about the problem. "I cannot explain away your vision completely . . . I can assure you though, that there is no reason to think that you have lost your reason." He put his hand to his mouth. "Pardon that terrbile play on words. I would say that this is a case of prerecognition; strange but in no way uncommon." He watched my face. "You still would be able to recognise the place if you were to see it in life?" I answered that I was sure I could. He pointed a finger: "Look out of the window Mr King, look over there – the road leading away to the next village: that if I'm not sadly mistaken, that is where you will see your workhouse, in real stone and mortar. It stands empty at present. The old man who owned it has been absent for some time and it has been rumoured that he may have passed away. How you dreamed up the image, without ever seeing it, is beyond the thinking power of a country parson, but God willing, there is a reason. I'll just say, God bless you and I trust I shall see you both again."

As we took our leave, I felt imbued with a new lease of life. Emma was alternating her walking with a little trot. "Harold," she gasped, "I haven't the shoes for this sort of pace; you'll have to slow down a bit." I laughed; I admit I was breathing heavily myself, and I altered my pace to suit Emma's.

"The Vicar was a dear, don't you think?" Emma panted. "Mind you, I don't believe in meddling with things I don't understand . . . and neither should you Harold."

The road began to go uphill. "Look dear, I probably saw an old photograph in my grandad's picture album. If his father was born in this area, he could have had photographs of some of the buildings in the village." Just as we were nearing the top of the hill I distinguished the object of my disquiet: The Old Workhouse. There it stood, more or less as I had pictured it.

Emma wasn't overjoyed when I told her that the place was just as I had seen it imposed on the leaflets. "I suppose it's a gift of some kind; I've read of such things, but I wouldn't have thought that you, Harold, a healthy businessman, would have been bothered with such fantasies." She was not unsympathetic in any way and this was her way of saying she was a trifle frightened by the progress of events.

Our chatter had brought us to the front of the workhouse. We stood there, outside the subject of our speculation. It was positioned right on the side of the road with no front garden nor gate. I imagined that the passage of time had seen various inroads into the property. Possibly there had been an entrance suitable to such a place, but the gradual widening of the road over the years had stripped the place of all accessories to grandeur: there it stood; a long, low, rambling pile of granite.

The house had an unmistakably neglected look. We stood there for a moment, then Emma went over to one of the lower windows, and holding her hand over the glass, tried to peer into the interior.

"I wouldn't do that love," I admonished.

"It's all right dear, there's nobody living here; it's empty."

As we were wondering what to do next, a voice sounded faintly from across the road. We turned around, to see an elderly woman leaning over a stone garden wall. "Be you lookin' at the ol' 'ouse me 'andsomes? 'Tis empty. 'Ers bin empty fer months."

"Is it for sale, do you know?" I asked.

The old person seemed not to have heard my question. "Belonged to ol' Mr Booth, poor lover; 'e were like small titties fer nigh a year, 'e were. Then 'e went an' died; never 'ad no kith nor kin he didn'; in the 'ands of they there lawyers 'tis."

Emma and I exchanged glances. The old woman certainly desired to have a conversation, and I was tickled by her Cornish talk.

She settled herself more comfortably, elbows on the stone wall, and regarded us with interest. "I got the keys, me 'ansomes, if you'm interested in lookin' round. 'Tis dirty, min' you." She turned, and went indoors; before we could decide whether she had lost interest and gone, she was out again holding a bunch of keys.

Emma smiled with pleasure; she loved looking at old houses; always had. "We would love to look in."

The old woman was out of her garden, and over the road in a trice, for this was adding spice to her day. She came up beside us, fumbling with the bunch of keys, "Yer 'tis," she said, holding up a huge key from among the lesser ones.

"Gracious," said Emma. "I've never seen such a big one."

The old woman seemed to straighten up with pride. " 'Tis ol' work'us key, my dearie; this were the ol' work'us years ago, afore my time. Didn' 'ave a good name they say. Them days is gone, thank Gawd; 'twas real hard in them days . . . no friends, ner money, an' that."

With those wise words, she slid past us, and turned the great key in the lock. The door protested at the intrusion with the traditional squeal, and we passed over the threshold. The air inside was dank and earthy. This was only to be expected, since the place had been uninhabited for twelve months or more.

The old woman kept close to us; it was obvious that she was far more interested in us than the house, which she had doubtless been in many times before. Mind you, I preferred her method of salesmanship, if you could call it that, to the commercial agent's – there was much more native wit in her comments. No, it was us she was curious about. We were emmets, the term used for strangers, the people who seasonally descend on the natives and alter their traditional life-style: those who fill the country lanes with evil-smelling motor vehicles, and who empty the local shops of the necessities of daily life.

While we were taking in all the good and bad points of the dwelling, the old woman was delivering an oration on the late owner. " 'E were carried out, poor ol' dear, on one of they there stretchers." She was enjoying herself immensely.

There was no hall, to speak of, the ceilings were timbered, and the rooms were comfortably large. Of course, the building had been altered. The ground floor consisted of a very large lounge, leading through an arch to the dining-room, which was open to the kitchen, reached by a single step the full width of the room. Emma cried out in delight as she spied an ancient but still impressive Aga cooker. The interior was rather dim however. Emma was in her seventh heaven. "Oh Harold, isn't this just divine! You must find out if it is for sale."

I was eager to admit that I liked the house as much as Emma. Despite the gloomy interior the place had potential.

The old woman was beginning visibly to lose interest. "I reckon you wants to look upstairs deary, though I can't stop much longer – Garge'll be home soon."

"We won't keep you more than a minute or so!" I exclaimed. Emma was running up the steps to the upper floor. I followed, mentally noting the stone steps, and thinking about a satisfactory covering.

"We must be going soon," I called to Emma. I shared her liking for the place. The upper floor had a bathroom en suite with the main bedroom, a couple of smaller bedrooms, and a shower-room and loo.

I turned back to the old woman. "Do you happen to know the name of the solicitors who have the property?"

She didn't seem to hear me. "Excuse me, you know – I never asked your name."

She heard me that time. "Oh 'tis all right me 'andsome; Gargett's the name; Nanny, they all calls me – Nanny Gargett." She smoothed the front of her frock and started again. "Yes, 'tis Wilcox and somebody or other. They lawyers always 'as to have one or two partners in crime; funny in't it? I reckon they'm no good on their own; don't reckon they'm any good anyway."

She cackled loudly and I began to lose patience.

"Where do they have their offices; do you know that?"

"Oh, that's Penzance, me dears," She went on "Oh I knew poor ol' Mrs Booth; yes, 'er were a nice ol' soul; kep' the place spick an' span 'er did; painted all black an' yellow it were then. When 'er died, the ol' man lost heart, poor dear, didn' 'ave the strength of a wranny . . . Now me dears, if you've seen all you wants . . ." She was edging us to the front door. We thanked her for her trouble, and I slipped her a pound note. We were marching briskly down the hill before she had taken the key out of the lock.

Emma could barely contain herself as we almost ran back to the bus stop. Then she let out a shout of glee. "I like it – no, I really adore it! Harold dear, don't you love it?"

I admitted to being very much impressed. "I'll write tonight, dear; there's no point in delay. If you like the place, then I'm bound to; but anyway, don't you realise we're ordained to have it?"

Emma was not quite sure about that.

We were back at the flat within an hour and before the night was out I had written my letter and decided to 'phone my lawyers in the morning. This I did, from my office, and my solicitor agreed to proceed with the purchase on my behalf.

I had the cash, so the preliminaries were not too complicated and the purchase was completed in about a month. We visited the house frequently; I suspect that Emma went on her own several times. We found life very full; my business was ticking over nicely and I had a good, efficient staff, so I had no worries there. Emma was full of plans for every room, and also she had to buy everything that was needed to furnish the place. By then I had bought a little car, so travelling presented no problem. During one of our first excursions to the house, Emma discovered a bonus we hadn't expected: on one of the lounge walls about three foot from the floor was an unusual painting. It's subject was simply a key, and it was not just a daub, but a masterpiece. I am not a connoisseur, but when a painting is almost three dimensional in its representation then it strikes me as a great work of art. God only knows who the artist was. Emma was entranced with it. She recognised it as a painting of the great front-door key and saw to it that no article of furniture obscured it. I 'phoned the lawyers, but they said that there was no mention of such a painting in the deeds – in fact, they were not particularly interested. I felt I had gained with the home a work of genius. Then Emma had a brainwave, that I should make a frame for it and fix it to the wall, giving the impression that the painting was actually framed. I liked the idea, but somehow never got around to it.

We had been in occupation about two months, it was bitterly cold and there was a lazy east wind blowing – the type that doesn't bother to go around you but straight through you instead. I had been hard at it, stocktaking, and arrived home tired and a bit on edge. However, Emma had cooked a delicious meal, and we had left the table well satisfied. In my comfortable carpet slippers I shuffled into the lounge, where Emma had built a roaring fire. I put a recording of Horowitz playing Beethoven's Moonlight Sonata on my music centre and slumped back in my big wingchair. Emma sat opposite me; she had chattered away so much during our meal that she had run out of subject matter. I was in no way displeased with this situation. The wall lights cast discreet, mellow illumination, vying with the fitful glow of fire, and over all this Beethoven cast his spell. This was Heaven, I mused. I picked up my Barling and filled it with my favourite Balkan Sobranie. Now this was complete bliss. Emma took up a book, but I watched it slowly slip from her grasp, and smiled indulgently. I looked up at the clock over the mantlepiece; it was eleven-thirty. I leaned across and touched her knee. Her eyes were wide open in a flash, and although not admitting to dozing off, she was anxious to get to bed. I said that I would see the fire out as it was low by now. I took the record off, as the last movement of the Sonata seemed a bit vigorous when I was thinking of slumber. Then I must have dozed off – I sat up with a start. The fire had died right down to a red ash, quite safe to leave. I went round the house downstairs to make sure the place was securely locked up. I was certainly half asleep as I started to go up the stairs ... But something was missing and I was suddenly aware of an urgent call from the recesses of memory. I looked around again and ... yes, the painting of the key was gone! 'Can't be,' I grumbled to myself. I would look in the morning; it was too late tonight. I turned again towards our bedroom. There was no reason to search for a painting which had to be there anyhow. Tomorrow I'd tell Emma the joke.

Reaching our bedroom door, I switched off the passage light. Emma was already fast asleep. I half thought of the key ... I'd leave the problem until the morning. I've always found this a good idea when confronted with a complex situation – leave it and sleep on it. I undressed slowly, and got into bed. To my chagrin, although the bed was warm and very comfortable, something was striving to alert my brain. I wanted to sleep, but this key business now kept cropping up. I sat up and reached for a book and put on my reading glasses. A little light reading I thought, by the soft glow of my bedside lamp ... No, I didn't want to read. I looked around the room: we had certainly made it a comfortable, cosy bedroom with its cream and gold furnishings, the harmonising Chinese carpet, and the full-length mirrors on the wall units. Still I couldn't sleep. Now, I am one of those people who must have a full night's sleep – I can't help it, but the very idea of insomnia frightens me. I got out of bed, and wended my careful way downstairs. I went over to the cabinet and poured myself a small glass of armagnac. As I put the bottle back I glanced at the wall ... No key. Can't help it now, Harold old chap, I told myself. I turned towards the stairs with my glass of armagnac, and slowly ascended again. I slipped into bed, glass in hand, Emma still sleeping the sleep of the just. Me? – I soon found that armagnac was not the drink to lull me to slumber. 'I'm back to square one,' I grumbled to myself. I peered over to the door, which I had left open. I always do, my bedroom door. I don't suffer from claustrophobia exactly, but I hate being shut up too much. I heard the rain, pit-a-pat, outside; the wind was rising too, but these were the normal voices of the season. Then, another sound intruded . . . and this was an alien sound. As I sat up in bed it seemed as though all my inner, hidden forces were striving to identify this sound. I hoped that it was a branch of a tree, brushing the glass . . . or was it water gurgling down the spout? No, those are innocent sounds, members of nature's orchestra. Something in my mind – or was it the armagnac? – assessed the sound, and believed it had something to do with the missing key. 'What rubbish!' shouted my conscious mind. But into my inner ear 'Wait, wait . . .' warned my subconscious. I did wait, with a degree of dread. My ears, straining to their limits, now identified a sort of – swish . . . swish . . . was not definably dreadful, yet it seemed to me almost unbearably sinister. There was nothing visible to give the sound more substance, but there was the unhealthy feeling that the sound was coming nearer. My brain was working frantically to bring commonsense to the rescue. All it achieved was to imply that the swishing sound was in a rhythm closely connected with the moving of feet! If it was footsteps then there had to be an intruder. I have never pretended to a great degree of courage, but in these circumstances I would defend my own. But now I was sure that the intrusion was not a physical one and sweat was tracing patterns down my face and neck. The door of the room had not opened more than I had left it, but something stood in that doorway, of that I was sure; yet I saw nothing . . . I only felt a chilling of my blood, in spite of the beads of sweat even then soaking the collar of my pyjamas. I knew that Emma, still sleeping blissfully, would blame the armagnac, but I knew better; I was certain-sure that the source of those sounds, evil as it had to be, regarded me as the intruder. The ordeal lasted no more than a few moments, but it seemed to stretch a whole horrible night.

In the morning I did not tell Emma anything about my experience. I just went down to the kitchen to make a cup of tea for us both. As I passed through the lounge, I glanced over at the wall: there was the painting of the key, just as it always was;

the same masterpiece. What a fool I'd have made of myself if I'd told Emma the key was missing! It showed how easy it was to imagine things. The darned thing had been there all the time! Of course it had. How could it have moved? 'Stands to reason,' I told myself. 'Or does it?'

I was rather preoccupied during breakfast, and Emma was quick to comment, "Are you feeling all right Harold dear?"

I mentally shocked myself out of a feeling of gloom. "Of course I'm all right, my love. Come to think of it though, I found myself in a bath of perspiration when I woke up; must be the start of a cold; I'll have to watch it."

"Look dear, why not just ring the office to say you're not well?"

I passed the whole thing off, glad that Emma had been satisfied with my excuses, by murmuring something about it being important that I be at the office today, as I had a new consignment of wines coming in. My day was indeed a busy one and I found no time even to think of my nightmare of the previous night. Emma had been busy during the day and on my return that evening could hardly wait for me to pronounce on her latest cooking venture, Cornish pasties. Whatever the native ones tasted like, I was delighted with hers. I made an attempt to rise from my chair, thinking the meal was over.

"Not yet Harold, you've really got to make room for another Cornish dish."

"Oh Emma, I don't think I could manage any more dear," I protested.

She took no notice instead bringing in a large dish with a pastry top; I eyed it with concern, but it turned out to be delicious blackberry and apple pie, topped with Cornish cream.

I felt dopey after all these goodies, but once in my own chair in front of the fire, I lit up my pipe and prepared to listen to Emma's detailed gossip about Gulval and its inhabitants.

She stood in front of the fire, a favourite position of hers, for she knows that I must look at her then, as I'm not able to see the fire. "Now Harold," she said. "I've found out quite a lot about this place." I waited. "Things that you and I never suspected." She saw a smile being born on my face. "I'm serious, Harold. This place is haunted!" She stopped, expecting some cry of horror or disbelief from me.

I just waved my pipe, in the manner of a conductor of an orchestra. "I know dear."

"You know?" she gasped, incredulity in her lovely eyes. "What do you mean Harold?" There was a tone almost of accusation in her voice.

"I mean; well, almost all older houses have that sort of reputation, haven't they?"

Emma was not to be fobbed off with that sort of answer. "Have you got some theory about this house then?"

I could see that she was really worried and tried to ease the situation by getting up and going to the wine cabinet to pour out drinks for both of us.

But Emma would not be diverted. "I suppose you are going to say something about your silly premonitions!"

I didn't care for that, so I told her straight about the nightmare.

She froze. "Why didn't you tell me Harold? I think it very wrong, to allow me to feel that this house was a lovely old place; and now you've ruined it." She burst into tears.

This I never could stand. "Look, Emma, you've just said the villagers told you that the house is haunted. Were you worried when they told you?"

She pouted: "That's different. Anyway, what are you going to do about it?"

"Do?" I exclaimed. "What do you expect me to do? – I never saw anything dear; I only kept the story from you because I thought you might worry."

"Worry? Of course I'm worried. Anyhow, I don't really believe in ghosts; it's only the thoughts that other people put into my mind that I don't like."

I went over to her and held her tightly in my arms. I tilted her chin up and kissed her. "There's no need to panic my darling" I murmured.

"I'll die of fright," she answered.

"You won't know; you didn't hear anything last night; you slept the whole night. If you're not psychic, you'll never suspect anything unusual." I was trying to gain time, feeling there had to be a reason for the manifestations I had experienced. Then I went on: "Look love, you have told me a thousand times how you love the old place; why not trust me? I'll work things out."

Emma looked at me doubtfully. "I know, I love the place, but . . ."

"No buts, my love; we have bought the house, and here we stay, come what may." I said that, but I lied in my teeth, for I was still afraid from last night.

Emma decided to have her drink. She was still troubled, but she always had trusted my judgement.

"I promise you, dear," I said, "that nothing here can harm you."

At last Emma agreed that I was probably right, as usual. We spent the rest of the evening forming a plan of campaign. I was to wake Emma, if I heard anything strange during the night, and together we could face whatever was about in the house.

When we were ready for bed, we both looked at the painting of the key. There it was, large as life, a fixture on the wall. We went up to bed, and slept like the proverbial top.

When I arrived at my office the next morning, Mrs Fowler, my secretary, asked how we were settling in. I replied that Emma and I loved it, but then for some reason I found myself telling her the whole story: the nightmare of the other night, the missing key; everything. As I told her about these things that we could not account for, I noticed that she was looking intently at me, so intently that I remarked on the interest that she showed.

She apologised. "I'm sorry Mr King, but before you started to tell me all this I knew that there was something amiss." She smiled, "You see, I'm what is called a medium, a person who has a gift, the power to read through the mists."

I was astonished, and showed it. "Do you mean to say, you can communicate with . . .?"

"Not in so many words, Mr King. It's true that I have been able to give solace to some who have lost a loved one, and I get premonitions, which I did in your own case, if you'll excuse me for saying so." I sat back in my chair heavily. "You mean that you believe all that I've told you, just like that?"

"Of course. Your mirages, as you called them, are part and parcel of a plan. This is my firm belief. You were meant to buy that house, and for what it's worth, I am sure that you will come out all right in the end."

"Well, thank you," I replied. "I agree that things tend to give that impression, but I can't see . . ."

She smiled. "You will. You yourself are psychic, though you don't realise it. Why do you think you heard the sounds, while your wife slept? Why do you think you saw the house pictured on every print you looked at, while your good wife saw nothing unusual? Many have the gift, and don't suspect it. You have little or no need of outside help. I can assure you that all these so-called hauntings are cries for help from something or someone who has had to stay behind, in the spirit. A job unfulfilled perhaps; nobody likes to leave a job unfinished . . . at least nobody who counts at all. So take heart Mr King; you and your wife must, and will, see this thing out to the end; as I said, you were ordained to buy that house, before you ever left your home thousands of miles away."

I listened flabbergasted, my mouth probably open most of the time. As she spoke she had taken off her glasses and polished them. Here was another revelation: Mrs Fowler with her glasses on was just another highly efficient private secretary; now without them, her eyes glowed like twin pools of wisdom – the natural wisdom of the ages. I felt that a man's life, if she desired to read it, would be as legible to her as an open book.

I wondered if those glasses were really an aid to vision, or were they to hide a power which could embarrass or shame anyone who looked into her eyes? As I stood aghast, she spoke again – I was hypnotised . . . The voice, like the eyes, had undergone a subtle change: "You have found a mystery . . ." There was a pause, as though the strange voice was having difficulty in reaching me, then: "The inner mind will solve all things. Something remains unfinished in the Workhouse . . . It waits for you . . ." The voice faded, but had not failed to give advice. Mrs Fowler was calmly doing what she had started to do before the change of voice came on her – she was still polishing her glasses. For my part, I had never experienced such a bizarre situation. This must have been clear to her, for she started to explain that she owed her clairvoyant powers to her Cornish forebears of the ancient family of Trease, many of whose members had been noted 'cunning' men or women, and who, despite the persecutions of the ignorant in a benighted age, had passed down their craft and knowledge from generation to generation.

I found my tongue at last: "I must say I've had a very strange but enlightening morning, even without a deal of actual business done," and I gave her a wink. "Thank you for your encouragement," I finished. And Mrs Fowler laughed – something I had not often heard her do.

After leaving the business at six, I determined to tell Emma all about Mrs Fowler and the strange voice. I hoped also that I would be allowed to solve the key mystery. The rain clouds were low and threatening as I drew up outside our house.

Emma was quickly out to greet me. "What have you been up to today?" I asked, while I hugged her tightly.

She grinned. "Most of the day wondering what to prepare for my lord and master's dinner."

As her eyes were dancing with mischief, I threatened to chastise her, and once indoors, started to chase her round the house. There was much screaming and laughing and I had to call a truce, as I said I was worried about the neighbours and what they might think. Emma roared with laughter: "Admit it, you beast, you're making excuses; you know you're winded. Carrying too much fat, that's what's wrong with you." To tell the truth, Emma was right; I was carrying more weight than I should; however, after we had both recovered from our exertions, Emma demanded that I do justice to her prepared meal. A dish that she had spotted in a new cookery book. What it was I've forgotten; suffice that it was like cottage pie, but a lot more delicious, and I complimented the cook.

After that repast, we cleared up between us, then retired to the lounge. Emma had stoked up a beautiful fire. I was not surprised when I heard a frantic drumming of rain on the windows, nor was I perturbed for we were snug and warm. I switched on a recording of Bach's D minor Toccata – What better accompaniment could one have to Nature's elemental orchestra? Emma went over and turned down the volume a bit; she prefers Strauss to the three Bs. I sat back and regarded with appreciation and affection the way she had decorated our rooms during my absence. While I am at business, she is probably either up a ladder with a paint brush or adding a heavy Indian rug here or there.

"Anything new at work?" she said.

I spent the rest of the evening telling her of my remarkable episode with Mrs Fowler. She let me carry on without interruption, though I knew she was bursting with questions. With Bach's great Fugue as a backcloth we discussed Mrs Fowler, and her story. Then Emma told me that she had met someone in the village, whose aunt had once stayed at our house in the days of Mrs Booth. Apparently she was a spiritualist, and had seen something during a night spent here. What she saw she never really explained, but the niece told Emma that it must have frightened the old soul properly. However, the person was dead now, so there was no chance of confirming anything.

Our chatter had gone on longer than our music, so Emma chose a suitable Chopin Nocturne, while we sat on either side of the great hearth. The rain and wind had eased by now, and the moon displayed a pale misty light. Emma's eyes were heavy; the sensuous warmth of the fire and the feeling of security made us both think of the room upstairs.

. "How about a nightcap?" I asked.

"Not for me dear," she replied, "I shall go off as soon as my head touches the pillow."

"Carry on sweetheart, I'll listen this record out and come up later."

I took off the Chopin disc, and was putting it away, when I thought I'd like to hear the last movement of Beethoven's Moonlight Sonata: the thundering chords would suit the weather's mood. Those lightning arpeggios spoke as much in music as ever Shakespeare did in words. After that, well satisfied with my day, I locked up and turned out the downstairs lights. I wended my way up the stairs, having forgotten the key and even the name Workhouse ... But that was only to last until the house, and one mortal in it, were at rest.

Emma was fast asleep when I entered the room. I went over to the little window and as I pulled the curtains apart to look out, I pondered on the mass of detailed work that Emma had put into the place. Her labours, when I was at work, had transformed a neglected old place into a real home. As I undressed I could see the dark night clouds greedily snatching at parts of the sickly moon as they raced each other across the sky. 'All's well,' I mused, as I sleepily kicked off my slippers, and slid into the warm bed. 'Ah' I grunted, as I settled down to a comfortable, dreamless night ... 'Damn!' I said to myself. 'I thought the key business was not to bother me tonight.' But alarm bells were jingling in my brain. 'I'll get no sleep, if I don't go down – Why am I pestered with this cursed key complex?' I tried to forget the whole affair, but no, I just had to go. I slid my feet into my carpet slippers, turned on the bedside light and warily made my way to the door. I was not yet able to walk confidently into the outer darkness; you have to live in a place for years to do that. With one hand outstretched, I gingerly felt my way to the stairs. Of course there was no eerie creaking, the stairs being of stone. Luckily for my foot comfort, we had managed to secure the carpet safely. I reached the lounge, and switched on the lights. I looked toward the wall which bore the key – and it was not there! No, no sign of the damned thing. All my feeling of confidence which hadn't been very strong anyway, vanished. I felt I was losing my grip on myself ... I was sane wasn't I? I was sweating now, and talking aloud fast. With hands brushing across the wall, I scanned it more thoroughly ... oh the key was gone, all right! Fear took charge. 'If this is to go on, without explanation,' I told myself, then my sanity will go with it.'

I ran up those stairs as though the powers of evil were close behind. 'The lights!' I stubbed my toes as I rushed to the bed, I cried out with pain, I clumsily knocked over a bedside chair – Emma woke with a start, her eyes wide, as I gasped, "That cursed key, it's gone again."

She recoiled in horror. "Don't go down again Harold, stay here with me please". She clung to me. "Leave it all till morning, do."

I got into my bed, my whole body shaking as though with ague. Holding her trembling body to me, I murmured, "Don't worry love, go to sleep again, I shan't move!" I waited, and Emma, now feeling more secure, dozed off quietly.

I thought to myself, 'It seems that I have to fight whatever this is, alone. Emma seems to be completely unware of the influence of the paranormal. It looks as though Mrs Fowler was right. I am apparently psychic.'

Even as Emma dozed in my arms, the room, our bedroom,

was disappearing. There was a strong smell of carbolic – the name came easily to mind: what did I know of carbolic? The very material presence of the vile stuff would ruin my wine tasting palate. It was incredible . . . I could not remember ever smelling this overpowering odour before – yet its name came to me just like that.

There was now another light in the room. Though weak, it had completely eliminated our own lighting. By this puny light I could see . . . not our cosy little bedroom but a long room; not a room, but a dormitory. The walls were rough stone, white-washed, and the windows naked to the elements. Unwillingly I looked further into the horrible room and in the dimness at the far end I could see rows of little iron bedsteads . . . God! This carbolic was getting stronger! Something warned me that if I couldn't smell the carbolic, then I would have to endure a nameless nausea, something more horrible. I writhed mentally, but somehow summoned the courage to continue my gaze. Of those pitiful beds, some at the extreme end were occupied; the others were laid out in a military fashion, as though for inspection. A minimum of rough sheets were folded over what seemed to be straw-filled mattresses. Sitting bolt upright on each bed was a woman. All of them seemed painfully thin, their ages impossible to guess since privation had robbed them of youth. The clothes worn by each pitiful figure were identical: shapeless dull blue ankle-length dress and white mob cap. Their footwear I could not see for their long dresses hid them. These garments were not of my generation, nor of the previous one.

The sight of this strange assembly was tearing something away from my mental energy. I felt the longer I watched the performance the weaker I was becoming. It was as if I had to contribute something in order to witness this ghostly progression, whether I wanted to or not. I had no will to return to physical credibility. Still I gazed on those hapless creatures, with their faraway resigned expression, victims – of what? Although I knew in my innermost being they were not of my era, that I was viewing something long past, I still felt intense sadness, mixed with repugnance and horror for these creatures, robbed of youth, and even worse, deprived of death! There they sat, waiting, waiting . . .

I could feel that this was not all I had to see. I knew – yes,
here it was – swish . . . swish . . . swish . . . Yes, I had heard the
sound before, but now there was vision too. Needle-pricking
stabs of fear pierced me, for now I could see the emanation
which caused that noise. It was a woman, and the sound I heard
was that of her voluminous skirts brushing the bare floor as she
marched in. Swish, swish. This figure was as plump as the other
poor souls were thin. And there it was – in her hand, the key. I
could see her face, hard as the very stone in the walls, her eyes
like agates. She surveyed the scene and I was at least grateful that
I was not in her vision, for her expression filled me with horror.

From her skirt pocket she took a piece of paper and holding it
up to read, she called out in a rasping voice – "Rosa Phelps?"

The answer came from one of the creatures: "Here, Mam."

Molly Gale?"

"Here, Mam."

She went on, getting a "Here Mam" from each, until she had
called seven names.

Then I thought the whole room was throbbing, or was it my
heart? I would have screamed, but my throat was constricted by
fear. God! This infernal throbbing! She called out an eighth
name, but there was no answer. The owner of that name was to
answer no longer.

Without any sign of emotion she called out a ninth and tenth.
They too were only corpses, past all her power. God, how I
hated all that I was seeing! Yet I was forced by a greater power
than I to watch this obscene charade. One good thing – though
I feared for my own reason, Emma was still sleeping like a child
in my now frozen arms. Still I continued to watch, as those
pitiful fragments of humanity formed into line at a command
from the woman with the key, and then passed through the door.
Gone, gone the assembly of the charnel house – but for the dead.

As the last one passed out through the door, I was once more
in my own bedroom, snug and secure in my own time, Emma
still sleeping at my side. I'd gamble that the key was now back
on the wall – just a painting.

I awoke next morning with a splitting headache. I went to the
bathroom and searched the cupboard until I unearthed the Alka-
Seltzers, dropped a couple in a glass, and half-filling it with

water, drank the potion off. I took a soothing shower, dressed, and went downstairs. It was still early. As I started to get the kettle for a cup of tea, I looked across to the lounge wall, *the* wall: there it was, the key. Dried and cracked with age, goodness only knows how long it had decorated that wall. I stared at it. What kind of modern science could explain this haunting? I felt a mad urge to scrape the paint from the wall – and I imagined a voice faintly but definitely saying, "Get rid of it, destroy it for God's sake!" But I pushed the whisper out of my mind. Was it reasonable? – to destroy a work of art because of a succession of nightmares? Was my impulse born of the pent up emotion of the previous night? I felt my hands go out toward the painting – Was I going to pander to a fancy – a waft of thought?

"What are you doing down there Harold?"

Emma's voice saved me from getting paint under my nails. I tried to pull myself together. "I'm brewing myself a pot of tea dear," I called out. Thoughts that had for a brief moment careered through my brain vanished into thin air, though, in a queer way, I seemed to feel rather than hear . . . a sigh.

Emma was full of good spirits, having had a fair night's sleep. On her way to the stairs to call me, she spotted a scrap of paper on the carpet. When I came into the lounge carrying a tray with the tea, she was reading the paper.

"What do you make of this?" she asked. She handed me the paper to read but as soon as I touched it, it dropped to the floor. "Butter fingers," laughed Emma.

No, the reason was that all the terrors of the night had come flooding back to me, for the paper reeked of carbolic. I put the tray down and shamefacedly picked up the sinister fragment. It was soiled, the writing yellow with age. I put on my reading glasses, for Emma's peace of mind. I already knew what was on that paper; I knew it was the paper I had seen in the hand of that odious woman, last night. As I held it I felt unclean. How it had materialised through the veil of time will always be beyond human understanding.

"What does it say, dear?" For some equally incredible reason Emma seemed unable to decipher the wording.

"It's just a list of names dear; we don't know them. I've no idea where it came from," I lied, for my wife's peace of mind. I read them out: "Rosa Phelps, Molly Gale . . ." It was like an obituary.

"Oh don't bother, love; they mean nothing to us." It was no bother, and I read out the rest – at least, I read until I came to the seventh name. Then my heart started to thud at an alarming rate. I had heard all these names called the previous night, but in my utter terror I had missed the significance of one. While all this was racing through my brain my face must have been a study of conflicting emotions. Emma put her arms around me, and begged me to tell her the reason for my obvious state of tension.

This made me decide that the time had come to tell her all that I had experienced, and what I thought of the crazy affair. I told her how I had found the key missing, which warned me of the bad night to come. I told her of the odious hag, who, clutching the key, read out a roll call from a scrap of paper, the same incredible paper that now lay on our breakfast table. Emma listened in horrified fascination. I related the pitiful procession of those unfortunates and their murmured replies to the woman, as she called their names. I even mentioned the mute trio lying as the Grim Reaper had left them . . . I told her all of it.

Emma started to sob. "What are we going to do, Harold? This is horrible! Why ever did we buy such a place?"

I didn't lose patience, because I knew she was right, but only up to a point, for the die was cast. There was too much coincidence, too many fingers pointing me towards the work-house. And there was the painted key, the trigger to the haunting. "Emma my love, please bear with me. Even if you could see what I have seen – and you don't seem to be sensitive, as they call it – then I promise you that no harm will come to you," I said as convincingly as I was able. This seemed to calm her and after a moment or two she went into the lounge to look at the painting. Without a word, she started to tug a small piece of furniture up to the painting, concealing it.

"Now," she said triumphantly, "let's see if she can find it!"

I laughed half-heartedly. "I hope you are right, love; but anyhow, when we are together, then we are safe – I hope." I said those last two words *sotto voce*.

We endorsed the statement with a good hug, which made us

both feel better. "We have to solve the mystery and cure the haunting," I said. "That's why I – we – have been brought here."

After breakfast I kissed Emma, and drove to the office. When I arrived I went through the personal mail, and then rang for Mrs Fowler. I invited her to sit down while I told her of the night's ordeal.

She was aghast. "What an experience!" she cried. "I'm sure though, that it bears out what I thought; that there is a definite connection somehow."

I showed her the scrap of paper.

"This is amazing." That was all she could say for a moment, while she examined it. "But you know, nobody would believe you. I do, though reason discounts such stories. Scientists tell us the world is composed of certain elements, and everything living, be it bird or beast, man or mouse, tree or orchid, all are composed of a combination of these elements. I cannot believe that the haunting has any bearing on you, and I am certain that you will one day be happy and secure in that same house. May I ask if it would be possible for me to call to see your wife, Mr King? I'd dearly like to see the house, if you don't mind."

I thought it would be a good idea for Emma to have a female companion to chat to, so I said "Why don't you come for the weekend, Mrs Fowler?"

She was visibly delighted. "Could I? I'd be pleased to come."

When she left my room, I phoned Emma to tell her that Mrs Fowler was coming for the weekend.

Emma had been eager to meet her.

"That'll be nice; I do get tired of wine prices and exports, etc. It'll be lovely to have a few hours of woman's talk for a change."

I knew the tone of mischief in her voice and called her a little hussy. At lunch time that day I visited the town library. There I inquired of an efficient young individual where I could find the area parish council records. He guided me to the reference section.

"What years are you interested in, sir?"

"Oh," I replied, "I'm thinking of records referring to the old Gulval workhouse."

He smiled, "It will take me a little while – about twenty minutes – that be all right?"

"Fine," I said. I walked over to one of the tables covered with current magazines but before I got interested in any of them the young man returned, laden with a bundle of dull green files.

"Hope you find what you're looking for here, sir; 1846–1882, back in the bad old days, I reckon, sir." He put the files on the table. "If you'll be good enough to pass them over the counter when you've finished, sir."

I thanked him, and proceeded to browse through the ancient pages. At first I found little beyond mentions of costs of council work and the like. I was beginning to get bored with it all when I spotted a paragraph on a subject of interest: the closure of the Gulval workhouse. With my heart in mouth, I read on. The date was 1880. 'Owing to high cost of proposed necessary repairs and modernisation, it was decided by a majority vote, to remove, and transfer the remaining inmates to Bodmin.' But that was not all; pinned to a survey map of the area was a note from a medical officer – I didn't know if such a paper should have been attached to those pages, but supposed the passage of time had robbed it of the confidentiality it would have had in 1880 – a note that for me solved the mystery of the three occupied beds in that accursed dormitary. It was a report, brief, but frightening. It read: 'March 5th, 1880. Called in by Matron of Gulval Parish Institution for the Poor [the workhouse]. I examined three inmates, all female. All had died of cholera. The bodies were removed, and straight away buried in a common pit which had been well laden with Quick-Lime. No burial service was performed, as it was deemed of greater importance, to prevent needless alarm to the populace.' There was also a hint that discipline in the workhouse was perhaps a little too rigid, more like that of a house of correction. The prime need for secrecy in the affair may have resulted in the eventual closure of the institution. Why Florence King had ended her days in such a place I shall never know.

Much pleased with my investigations, I went back to the office. Just before five o'clock Mrs Fowler appeared, dressed for the occasion. We were quickly at our door when Emma came out to greet us, having heard the car. Once introduced, the two

were soon chatting away as though they had known each other
for years.

Mrs Fowler's main interest was the painting of the key. While
we stood looking at it, she admitted that she was no judge of
painting, but, like Emma and me, she was impressed by the sheer
reality of the work. "If that had been painted on a canvas, I
would say that it would fetch a good price in an auction room."

I agreed grudgingly, as I almost feared the presence of it these
days, or I suppose I should say, the absence of it.

Emma had prepared a fine meal for us all. Later, we went into
the lounge, where Emma had an excellent fire going. We sat
chatting about South Africa and the old Commonwealth. Each
of us seemed reluctant to bring up the subject that we were all
anxious to see the end of. The weather was deteriorating, and
with the dark came driving rain and a high wind. After a
nightcap of armagnac we discussed sleeping arrangements;
although we had a pleasant spare bedroom ready, I mentioned
that we had a couple of sleeping bags which we might find
useful, if there was to be a repetition of the previous night's
experience. Mrs Fowler said that if such a thing happened again
that night, then she certainly wanted to be with us at the time.

We all went over to the wall with the painting. Again, it was
not there. This was the first time that Emma had witnessed the
disappearance of the key. She started to shake, apprehension
showing in her face. "Oh Harold, are you sure we can endure
this awful business? – I'm frightened; it's too much to expect, to
sit and wait for this evil thing!"

Mrs Fowler put her ample arm around Emma. "If you didn't
see anything when the key was missing before, then I doubt if
you will experience anything much. Mr King has been able to
endure it so far. Forewarned is forearmed, they say."

I apologised to Mrs Fowler, "You know, I feel a very poor
host, to suggest such meagre hospitality as a sleeping bag."

"Don't fret yourself on that score, Mr King; you know how
I begged you to let me come along, and I simply have to be
present if anything does occur tonight."

Emma shivered. "I simply don't understand how you can
willingly face a haunting. As Harold says, I just go to sleep, and
when I sleep, I'd sleep through anything . . . I think."

The tension eased with our light banter over the sleeping
bags. We had two very large high-backed basket chairs, which I
had bought cheaply in an auction room, as I had planned a home
for them in a little patio we would build next to the house. I
decided that these would be ideal for our vigil. I brought up
some cushions from the lounge, and Mrs Fowler took one
sleeping bag, while Emma and I, with much struggling managed
to fit ourselves into the other. I left the bedside light on, while
a small electric fire took the chill off the room. Then we waited.
The weather was worse, if anything. The wind was gale force;
the rain, driving against the window, sounded as if a giant were
throwing huge handfuls of dried peas against the glass. Mrs
Fowler had settled comfortably into her bag. Emma and I . . .
well, we simply had to huddle together to fit into the bag. With
my arms around her, the warmth was already sending Emma
into a fitful sleep, showing her touching confidence in me. For
myself I didn't feel too good. I wasn't looking forward to a
repeat of what I had seen before.

Then . . . a change? Yes . . . nothing to see, mind you, but a
tenseness already mounting. I noted that Mrs Fowler was alert
to the feeling, looking wide-eyed. Then the lights started to
surrender to a dim primitive set of oil lamps and I could just see
these puny outriders of the haunting, their fitful glimmer
revealing more shadows than forms. My nose wrinkled at a faint,
but growing smell . . . carbolic! Whitewashed walls, a bare black
hole, the frameless windows . . . God, but it was cold! That
carbolic, struggling in vain to conquer the sickly odour of
corruption . . . and now, on the bare boarded floor, I could see
the beds, their starkness mocking sleep; ten of them I could see
now. The ghostly parade was about to commence, in its pitiful
repetition. I could no longer see Mrs Fowler, nor Emma, nor
myself! We were not of this evil carnival. But wait; my ears, my
skin, could detect the malevolence. Swish . . . swish . . . that evil
rustle of heavy skirts brushing the bare boards; a clink, clink of
keys, the great key among them. She was in the room. Silence.
Seven figures were bolt upright at their bedsides, waiting. No
paper to call from, this time – I got a certain meagre satisfaction
out of that; I had the paper, out of her time; she couldn't touch
it; for it was in my trouser pocket. But there was no need of list;

this grim virago knew it by heart. By heart? What am I saying?
– She had no heart! Her voice rasped out "Rosa Phelps?" Each
inmate answered when her name was called. I listened; I don't
believe I was breathing as I waited for the seventh name.
"Florence King?" She called it and it was then that I forced all
my powers of concentration upon this young-old girl-woman.
There she was, my great-grandfather's sister! As young as Emma
– older by far – God Almighty, she was languishing in this hell
hole, this pest-house, when he, dear brother, was basking in the
African sun! The other three names were called: no matter there,
for they were safe from the harridan who forced the others to
their eternal repeat performances.

During this horrid charade I was going beyond my powers,
calling with my very soul: "Florence ... Florence ... look at
me," though I was sweating with fear. The omen of evil was
freezing my resolve, yet still I managed to find a last ounce of
latent spiritual energy to break into that malignant web. I knew
that I was shouting aloud – I was frantic – "Florence! – Please
look at me, in the name of God!" It had no effect, yet I kept on
... and then at last the seventh inmate looked towards me! By
the love of God, she saw me, across three generations, across a
hundred years of our time – not hers; time had ceased to exist for
her – she saw me as plain as I saw her. I was as near insanity as
I shall ever be, still I kept on trying to reach her, to strengthen
a bond whose only basis lay in a family tree. How I yearned to
see a change in her countenance. That was not to be, even
though a greater power than mine had enabled me to get a
vibration from our living world into that devilish parade of
death. There seemed no way that the performance, repeated
untold times, could be altered one whit, yet over that gap of
time she had surely seen, in the same manner that I saw her, one
of her own breed.

The cold in that cursed place was almost unbearable, yet
Emma slept on. I still could not see Mrs Fowler. I had only my
own eyes and ears. The other power was only loaned to me, of
that I'm certain.

The parade moved to the door, that disgusting hag waiting
for each poor earthbound creature to pass out into the passage. I
was straining, almost stretching out my hand, in a vain hope.

The first, second, third, passed . . . until the seventh. Then I saw a small handkerchief fall to the floor. The face turned slowly in my direction, the mouth moved – What powers were being used or called upon, in order to achieve these deviations from the century-old parade of the possessed? – and her message came across to me, though I'll swear on any bible that I didn't hear the voice – how could I? No, I *felt* the petition from a soul in constant torment: "In God's name . . . destroy the key . . . the key . . ."

How can I know that shadow, once Florence King, had even seen me? I can't. As always before, when the last figure had passed through the door, then the haunt was over . . . until the next disappearance of the painting. But this time I was determined that the message – that supplication from an almost lost soul – had to be, would be carried out, and by me alone. I was resolved there would be no more performances of that satanic ritual. Tonight would be the last night; or I would be a dead man. I had been pushed past my limit.

I sprang out from that sleeping bag, and ran to the window, throwing it open. The night air came rushing wildly into our bedroom. Thank God for the real cold air, fresh and pure! And the real things of our own time quickly reshaped, as though some invisible curtain had been pulled back to bring us back to comfort and security. Me? I was like a man possessed: all the pent-up emotions that fought the influence of the nightmare were breaking any self-control I had left. I rushed to the spot where the little piece of linen lay – yes, I had not dreamed it. It had been dropped, and on one corner were the neatly stitched initials: F. K. The world won't believe that – ever. I don't care – I have it. I'll never show it; it is too precious for other eyes; it is my private assurance of the next world – the other side – call it what you will.

Mrs Fowler and Emma were recovering in their own ways. I? I was still in a very abnormal state. I tore down the stairs, mouthing cries of rage, fear, hatred. I was insane, no doubt of that; insane in a terrible surge of feeling. I turned on all the lights in the lounge and searched. I was right: there it was, there, on the wall, the accursed painting of the key – that work of great art, that piece to be acclaimed by any connoisseur, what I now knew to be a malignant scab. I knew what I had to do. Shouting and almost frothing at the mouth, I searched for a suitable weapon. "Ah" I roared, spotting the fire shovel. I dashed over to it and armed with this tool I frantically hacked and scraped at the cursed thing – that evil anchor which had been the tool of the Devil's servant, that had held those hapless souls in torment for a hundred years. I screamed and swore luridly, my lungs at bursting point. I knew then that I had tapped a potential energy of purpose which all possess, but rarely if ever find the secret of tapping. In my mad energy I was ruining the wall surface for a square yard around. Lumps of masonry now were falling in chaotic and dusty array around my still bare feet.

I was still at it when Emma and Mrs Fowler appeared. They were fully dressed. Emma froze in horror. "My God, Harold my poor dear . . ." She rushed to my side and dragged me, still grimly holding a now battered fire shovel, away from the wall. Mrs Fowler stood apart but obviously concerned. I say this now, but at the time I was still fully under the spell of a self-appointed duty – to destroy that evil. It was in answer to a prayer in the name of God, and who was I to disobey?

While Emma went to bring a dustpan and brush to clear up some of the debris I felt a glimmer of sanity coming back, and self-control. I was able to give Emma a sort of smile, almost in triumph. Then I gently pushed her aside, and while the two bewildered ladies watched, I went out into the yard, and brought in a refuse bin which I proceeded to fill with the debris. Then I carried it out into the garden and carefully picked out every portion that had even a fragment of paint on it. I poured paraffin over the heap, and set light to it. I stood there, arms folded, watching the last act in my labour of purging. As the paraffin ignited the paint, for a moment the smell was masked by the malodorous stench of the charnel house. I was forced to retreat from the blaze: the blue cloud of tainted smoke rose high, there was a final whiff of carbolic, and it was gone!

Thank God, the air in the garden was so fresh and clean! I came indoors to find Emma and Mrs Fowler had been hard at work in my absence, Mrs Fowler having persuaded Emma to leave me alone while I was in my frenzied nightmare state. All that remained of my animal-like attacks on the wall were the unsightly pits in its surface. The floor and carpet were un-disturbed. Myself? – I was a man drained. I had spent energy – energy which might have sufficed for months of normal living. Now I would have to pay. Emma, love and concern showing in her eyes, helped me to a chair, and I really needed that help.

For nearly twelve months I needed care. My experience had been a searing one, but I was sure, and still am, that Great-Great-Aunt Florence had been able to contact me – our spirits had met. Those sinister roll-calls, repeated perhaps for a hundred years, were never to recur. Those pathetic shadows, spiritually beaten to evil repeat performances by that harridan from Hell, were now free to rest at last.

When I was able to return to my business, I found that Emma had got workmen in to redecorate our home. Mrs Fowler, too, had been a tower of strength. All this is now history. There have been no further visitations of any kind. Emma and I had long since agreed that we must have been ordained to spend our days in this old house. We love the place, anyway. I feel that I dearly have earned the right to live here and enjoy it. My task completed, we sometimes talk calmly about those terrible times. We have not replaced the work of art on the wall – I doubt whether either of us would greatly appreciate anything of the kind.